THE PURSUIT

A Spy Romance

MADHURI TAMSE

Photo Credit: Licensed from Adobe Photo Stock
Book Cover: Lumimagin (Sneha Designs)
Editor: Sejal Shah Srinivasan
Alpha Reader: Kavita Wadnerkar

BLURB

Trisha Chaudhary is a daring ex-RAW agent chasing criminals when a chance encounter in a nightclub washroom brings her face-to-face with the charming and intriguing *Krish Rajvanshi.* Unbeknownst to her, he is the powerful director of an elite global law enforcement organization - GLEN. After witnessing her impressive combat skills, Krish extends an invitation for Trisha to join his covert team. Though initially hesitant, she accepts, setting the stage for electrifying missions where their professionalism is tested by an undeniable attraction. Sparks fly as they attempt to deny their magnetic pull while tackling high-stakes operations against international smugglers and deadly cartels. But amidst these life-threatening crises, will they discover just how deeply they've come to rely on each other? Will the thrill of the chase finally give way to the allure of forbidden romance? Can they protect their hearts while taking down ruthless criminal networks?

A pulse-pounding tale of espionage and sparks of passion, ultimately culminating in a journey to love.

<u>Note from the Author</u>

Although this Book can be read as a Standalone, Krish and Trisha (the lead characters of this book are already introduced in another Political Romance Series of mine (The Gamble, The Maze, The Checkmate).

Paperbacks Out

It will always be a Bonus if you read that series first before reading this book. Nevertheless, if you want to dive straight into this Spy Romance, here you go…
I hope you love it.

CHAPTER 1 (FIRST MEET)

TRISHA

<u>Three Years Back</u>

The pulsating beat of the music reverberated through the walls of *Inferno Fusion Nightclub*, each thump syncing with the rhythm of the crowd's collective heartbeat. It was the weekend, and the club was alive with an electrifying energy that drew in Delhi's youngsters like a magnet.

The crowd was a sea of faces, each one lost in the music, surrendering to the rhythm of the night. As I weaved through the packed dance floor, bodies swaying and lights flashing, my eyes scanned every face I looked at, waiting to spot the one I was here for. The bar counter was bustling with activity, the laughter and chatter merging with the melodious tunes that echoed around me.

Dressed in black jeans and a full-sleeved button-down cream satin shirt, neatly tucked into the waistband, I felt the gentle brush of the fabric against my skin as I pushed the crowd to move ahead. The V-neck highlighted my neckline, an intentional decision to seamlessly blend into the vibrant crowd without arousing any suspicions that I had a different agenda than the carefree people around here enjoying their lives to the fullest. I never had the desire to live the kind of lives they did. My purpose in life was defined the very day I turned 21 and was selected to be a part of one of the best foreign intelligence agencies in India to monitor the activity that affects national security. Although I was no longer a part of that agency anymore, my purpose was still the same—fighting against the lawbreakers.

With my dark hair pulled back into a ponytail, I moved with purpose, the urgency in my steps hidden beneath the facade of someone out here for a good time. Handsome men attempted to approach me, drawn by the enigmatic aura, but my steely glance kept them at bay. Ignoring their advances, I focused on my mission, determined to find the man I was here for. The earpiece, nestled discreetly in my ear, was my lifeline, a connection to the unseen but ever-watchful eyes of my team who were here and monitoring the club like me.

"Any eyes on the target?" I whispered into the microphone concealed beneath my collar, my voice drowned out by the thumping bass.

"Negative." The reply crackled in my ear.

Gritting my teeth in frustration, I pushed my way through the crowd of dancing bodies. Every beat of the music fuelled my determination, and every flash of coloured lights heightened my senses. I was on a mission—chasing the son of Mumbai's famous drug cartel amidst the chaos of the nightclub. We had received a tip that he was here every weekend to have fun.

"Team Alpha, I'm checking the restrooms," I declared, striding purposefully toward the men's facilities.

"Trisha, cool down. Give me five minutes; I'll join you to check the restrooms," Paul urged.

I dismissed Paul's suggestion with a quick shake of my head.

"Five minutes is all it takes to jeopardise this entire mission, Paul. I'm going in." Asserting my decision, I swung my foot, kicking the restroom door open before marching inside.

"What the f*ck—" A man screamed aloud. He had just finished his business and had thankfully zipped up his expensive suit pants before glaring at me in disbelief.

The guy in front of me was the definition of eye candy—tall, handsome and well-built with a square jaw that could probably cut glass. My eyes couldn't resist lingering for a moment, making a mental note of every detail, from his piercing eyes to his perfectly styled hair.

"What nonsense is this? You can't be here, miss. It's a men's washroom," he insisted, breaking the spell.

"I know," I replied nonchalantly, dismissing his concern and continued scanning the rest of the area. The washroom was spacious, with several private doors lining the walls.

In an abrupt fit of annoyance, he marched over to me. "What do you mean, you know?" His anger was palpable, but I had a mission to complete.

"I'm looking for someone here," I stated matter-of-factly, not bothered by his intrusion.

The man seemed taken aback.

"What was so urgent that you couldn't wait for that 'someone' to finish his business here in the washroom and come out? Oh wait..." he chuckled. "That someone is your boyfriend or fiancé, right? And you suspect he is here with another woman, doing the other kind of business, right?"

I scrunched my nose at his bizarre guess and glared at him. "You find this funny, Mr...?"

"Krish Rajvanshi," he replied with a wink. "And no, I don't find this funny, but you were a second away from making it awkward had I not zipped up on time. And so what if I am a man. I still don't like strangers taking a peek when I am doing 'my thing,' you know?"

I rolled my eyes in anger. "I don't have such fantasies either. Wash your hands and get out of here," I scolded him.

It was then that Krish realised he hadn't washed his hands. He chuckled again. "Good observation. But whether I wash my hands or not is my problem, and walking out of here or not is my wish. I have the freedom to be where I want to be."

"Fine!" I screamed. "Then be here, but don't interfere in my business." I pushed him away to check the other doors, leaving him alone. It wouldn't affect him, but a minor error could jeopardise my entire mission tonight, a risk I couldn't afford to take.

I was about to push one of the many doors inside the washroom to check if the man I was pursuing was hiding there, when the same door swung open abruptly, and the very man I was here for shoved me behind and ran towards the exit. I stumbled, but Krish caught me at the right time.

"Stop," I screamed, but before I could act, the man locked the washroom door from the outside, trapping Krish and me inside. I banged on the door in vain, frustration building with every futile attempt. Krish, still in a state of shock, laughed at the absurdity of the situation.

"Was *he* your boyfriend?" he teased, enjoying my mess. "Poor guy! What have you done to scare him this much?"

I ignored his taunts and kept trying in vain to open the door. Krish looked seemingly entertained as he washed his hands and offered to help.

"Should I try?" he asked with a mischievous glint in his eyes.

My anger made me reject his offer.

"Don't mess this up more for me. Just move away," I snapped, my patience wearing thin as I kicked the door again in irritation.

Krish, undeterred, continued his playful banter, leaning against the wall next to the door.

"Let me guess, he's two-timing you. That's why you're so pissed off. Or he's ready to marry someone else because of family pressure and is dumping you. Actually, in both cases, I don't think he's worthy of a strong woman like you. You'll find better men than him. All you have to do is look around. Do you believe in serendipity? Like meeting someone who could be your forever, in a completely unexpected place… like a men's washroom?" he teased.

Enough was enough. I stopped kicking the door, gripped the lapels of Krish's suit and pinned him to the wall. Stunned by my move, Krish met my gaze, his lips parting in shock as I reprimanded him up close.

"Shut the f*ck up. He's not my boyfriend; he's the son of a drug cartel. I was chasing him for months. And because of you, I've lost focus and missed my chance."

"You lost focus because of me?" Krish grinned, undeterred by my anger. "Women only tend to lose their focus around irresistible men. So does that mean you find me irresistibly charming?"

I gritted my teeth, momentarily forgetting the dire situation, and scanned his face. Although he was getting on my nerves, there was something about this man that I could not pinpoint. He was funny and mysterious, too, and was completely unaffected by why I was here. He was so not my type. Yet, there was something about him which made me look at his handsome face more than once. But he didn't have to know that. So, with a nod, I replied to his previous query, "Charming fool."

Another grin popped on his face at my reply, but that very instant, the door I was trying to break was pushed open, and three strong men barged inside, escorting the drug cartel's son who had locked us up here. He had brought reinforcements to deal with me. Krish and I exchanged glances, instantly alert.

Even as the men advanced toward them, Krish managed to maintain his teasing demeanour. "Well, well, well. It looks like your charming fool needs to help you out. Should I negotiate your release with these gentlemen?"

I shot him a doubtful glance. "Get out if you don't want to lose your life. These men are dangerous." I stepped behind, trying to find a way to rescue Krish and me from this situation. Whatever it be, I am not letting a civilian get hurt, nor am I leaving this place without arresting the drug cartel's son.

"Are you sure you don't need my help? I can fight at least one, if not all three," Krish teased again.

Damn! Who was this man? He wasn't even scared for his life. Why was he even interested in getting into my mess?

"Trisha," the drug cartel's son leered, taking my name lasciviously. His laughter echoed in the background, blending with the pulse of the nightclub beyond the door, which he had locked again to ensure no one interrupted us. "You think you can still arrest me? These men are going to love breaking your bones."

"And I would love breaking yours," I retorted, lunging forward to fight his men, turning this confined space of the washroom into a makeshift battleground.

The first thug came at me, and I sidestepped his attack, landing a swift kick to his midsection. Krish, surprisingly joined the fight, taking on another assailant. I didn't know he could fight. His unconventional, unorthodox fighting style threw the men off guard, buying us a moment of advantage.

My training kicked in, and I dodged a punch, retaliating with a series of precise strikes on the attackers who kept lunging at us.

"Watch out," I shouted at Krish, who ducked at my warning, then swiftly turned around and kicked the man who tried to attack him from behind. His agility and resourcefulness shocked me to the core. How could he fight so well? Who was he? Together, we fought as an unlikely duo against the imminent threat.

Soon, the three hired attackers of the drug cartel's son struggled to fight back, their energies quickly dwindling. That's when the drug cartel's son decided to take matters into his own hands. He lunged at me with a frenzied determination, fuelled by rage and desperation. I dodged his attacks, while Krish, though not a trained agent, showcased an uncanny ability to subdue the rest of the men.

After what felt like an eternity, I finally managed to secure a hold on the drug cartel's son while Krish restrained the others. The door was kicked open, and my men and the local police entered the washroom. I took a sigh of relief, finally realising that the mission I was here for had succeeded.

"You okay, Trisha?" Paul asked, and I nodded at him, still breathing hard. "Good job," he added, equally relieved.

As my men dragged the attackers and the drug cartel's son out, Krish returned to me. He was about to touch me when I stepped back, confused by his sudden display of affection.

"Stop fussing. I've washed my hands, if you remember," he playfully chided before guiding me toward the basin and turning on the tap. The cool water flowed, a stark contrast to the heat and tension that lingered in the air.

With a dampened tissue, he tenderly touched my forehead, where a cut, unknown to me, had been silently oozing blood. Krish's touch was surprisingly gentle, leaving me momentarily breathless.

"So, Trisha, huh?" he inquired, his tone taking on a softer note now that he knew my name. As he cleaned the wound, his touch felt warm and comforting, and a subtle chemistry seemed to ignite between us. "Narcotics Control Bureau, CBI, state police...? Who do you work for?"

"It's none of your business," I retorted, perhaps a bit harshly, as I snatched the tissue from him, attempting to regain my composure. Although I tried to keep a distance, an unspoken connection lingered, an invisible thread that seemed to pull us closer. The touch of his fingers on my forehead had sparked something beyond the physical — a connection that hinted at the possibility of more encounters and more shared moments amid the unpredictability of our lives.

"Next time, don't get involved in my mess. You may lose your life," I warned him. Unable to handle this tension, I was about to turn around and leave, but he interrupted me.

"Next time?" he teased, his expression a mix of amusement and genuine curiosity. "You look quite interested in meeting me again."

I shot him a sharp glance, my attempt at seriousness meeting his persistent playfulness. "This isn't funny. It was a dangerous mission, and you shouldn't have been a part of it."

Unfazed, Krish leaned casually against the wall, a mischievous smirk playing on his lips. "Well, dangerous or not, you have to admit, it was a memorable first meeting, at least for me. Whenever I would use a public restroom henceforth, there would always be a lingering concern about my privacy, hoping you don't barge in there again, looking for your suspects."

I rolled my eyes, unable to hide a grudging smile. Krish possessed an incredible ability to turn a potentially tense situation into light-hearted banter, a skill that left me momentarily disarmed.

"Good," I nodded, feigning satisfaction. "I'm glad to leave that kind of impact on a man who thinks he's the coolest guy in the world."

I exited the washroom, knowing Krish had followed me out, too. I couldn't shake the feeling that Krish, with his charm and curiosity, had left an indelible mark on a mission that was supposed to remain strictly professional. Paul exchanged a glance with me, raising an eyebrow, silently questioning the unexpected ally by my side. Ignoring his unasked question, I stepped out of the neon-lit ambience of the Inferno Fusion Nightclub. Little did I know, our paths were bound to cross again, and the unpredictable journey had only just begun.

A month later, I received an offer letter from GLEN, the Global Law Enforcement Network, an organisation headquartered in Austria dedicated to combating international crime and tracking down the world's most wanted and elusive criminals. The letter extended an invitation for me to work as their secret agent in India for specific missions. What caught my attention was the signature on the letter, signed by one of its Directors—Krish Rajvanshi!!

In an instant, I realised he was the same man who had left a lasting impression on me since our initial encounter. Because beneath his signature, there was a personal handwritten note that read, *'Your charming fool.'*

Though the offer letter had caught me off guard, I neatly folded it with a smile playing on my lips, marvelling at how that day Krish had asked me if I believed in serendipity. It never crossed my mind that someone as charming and amusing as Krish could hold the position of Director in one of the world's topmost law enforcement organisations. Only a fool would give up on such an opportunity. Thus, I made the decision to accept it. After all, he had piqued my curiosity too and I wanted another chance to meet him and get to know him better. Period!!

CHAPTER 2 (SILENT SPARKS)

KRISH

The plane touched down in Delhi, and the familiar rush of anticipation surged through me. It had been four long months since that unexpected encounter in the nightclub washroom, and I was back in the city for some paperwork. But truth be told, my main agenda was to check on Trisha.

As I steered through the bustling airport, memories of our first meeting played in my mind like a well-scripted scene. The way she barged into the men's restroom, looking for suspects, was etched in my memory. Her combat skills and the precision with which she completed her mission—it all left me curious about this enigmatic woman.

Within two weeks, her entire life story was neatly compiled on my desk. An ex-RAW agent, currently working undercover with the state police—Trisha was no ordinary woman. She was smart, capable, and perfectly suited for a role in GLEN. I couldn't bear to let someone like her waste her talents on local police cases.

Most intriguing of all, there was an inexplicable pull, an attraction that I felt towards her. As the director of a powerful international organisation, I had encountered many women, but none had left an impression as she did in just one meeting. And the fact that she managed to do it without even trying made her all the more captivating. She had to be special.

A week after I sent her the offer letter, news of her acceptance reached me through my channels within Delhi's GLEN office. She started her training, both physically and intellectually, for the Global Law Enforcement Network, while I was back in Austria juggling responsibilities.

Despite my own demanding missions, I had kept a keen eye on her progress. Trisha excelled in every test—proof of her sharp mind and strong character. It was today, after four long months, that I would finally get a chance to see her again in action during her final physical test.

I arrived at the GLEN training facility, a secure compound hidden away from prying eyes. This was the place where new joiners from India were trained for the missions. The energy within the complex was electric. Agents in training moved with purpose, each step bringing them closer to becoming a part of a covert force that fought against international threats.

Trisha, clad in tactical gear, was in the midst of her final test. Three highly trained agents stood before her, formidable opponents for anyone to be taken down. I stood behind the glass wall of the room. As the director, my presence went unnoticed by most, allowing me to observe the unfolding scene without interruption.

Trisha fought with grace, a lethal combination of calculated strikes and evasive manoeuvres. Her movements were efficient, showcasing the result of months of intense training. It was clear that Trisha wasn't just meeting the standards; she was surpassing them. With each forceful strike against her opponent, she was delivering powerful blows to my heart which had been echoing her name ever since our first encounter.

As the physical test reached its end, she faced off against the three opponents simultaneously. The air crackled with tension as more blows were exchanged. It was a display of skill and determination that left me in awe. I couldn't help but marvel at Trisha's prowess.

"Impressive," I muttered to myself, a wry smile playing on my lips. The woman had an uncanny ability to leave me both intrigued and captivated.

The final blows were dealt, and Trisha emerged victorious. Beads of sweat adorned her forehead, and yet, there was a fire in her eyes that hadn't dimmed. As the agents dispersed, I finally stepped forward, revealing my presence.

"Trisha," I greeted with a subtle smirk on my face. "Well done."

She turned towards me, a mix of surprise and recognition in her eyes. "Director," she acknowledged, her gaze steady.

We had much to discuss—missions, strategies, and perhaps, the undeniable spark that had grown between us during these months of separation. The room felt quiet, leaving only the two of us in there. The moment our eyes locked, time seemed to stretch into an infinite moment, as if the universe itself had conspired to bring us together. Her gaze, intense and unyielding, held mine in a silent conversation that needed no words. Her eyes spoke volumes — enough to tell me that something deeper was brewing in her heart just as it was in mine.

Reality crashed back when she blinked, breaking the spell. Neither of us had moved, as if afraid that the slightest movement would shatter this fragile moment.

"What brings you here, Director?" she asked carefully, maintaining the professional line between us.

"Director?" A playful grin tugged at the corners of my lips as I replied.

"The last time I recall, you called me something else — a charming fool."

Trisha's smile, though hidden, sparkled in her eyes. "First impressions can be wrong."

I chuckled.

"But you superseded my first impression about you. That was one great fight you put against our strongest agents."

She wiped the sweat from her face, a casual gesture that spoke volumes about her strength and composure. "Thanks for the opportunity to be a part of such a huge organisation. I would never have dreamed of it even otherwise."

"You deserved to be here," I replied unable to help myself from admiring her a bit more — not just for her combat skills but for the layers beneath her formidable exterior. As the director, I had seen many agents, but Trisha was different — a unique blend of strength, skill, and an enigmatic charm.

"Thank you once again."

"Thank you with a cup of coffee sounds sweeter," I teased, unable to resist the playful banter. "I won't mind if you ask me out for a coffee today. Actually, I'm dying for a good caffeine fix right now to ease my jet lag."

She rolled her eyes, trying to hide her smile.

"In that case," she stepped behind. "I'll ask someone to bring you a strong coffee to keep you awake, Director."

Without missing a beat, she turned and walked towards the door, a deliberate retreat from the uncharted territory of unspoken feelings.

I stood there, grinning like an idiot, knowing full well that Trisha wasn't going to let her guard down so easily. Professionalism was her armour, and a coffee date with the director either didn't fit into her schedule or, perhaps she was purposefully avoiding it. Whatever the case, the mysterious pull between us had just begun, and I was more than eager to see where it would lead us in the near future.

TRISHA

A week had passed since Krish's arrival. Despite his position as the director and the almost-boss, Krish hadn't stopped being the charming, flirty man he was. His attempts for a coffee date lingered in my mind, a playful proposal that I deliberately avoided, knowing well enough that he wasn't going to give up that easily either.

I still lived in the training facility at GLEN, like a few other agents, until we were assigned our real missions. And in this one week, I observed Krish's relentless dedication to his responsibilities. Meetings with agents, technical briefings, and mountains of paperwork on an undisclosed mission—he handled it all with finesse. Yet, amidst the serious affairs of the law enforcement world, our eyes met at unexpected moments, creating a magnetic tension neither of us dared to explore further. Each encounter left us catching each other in the act. At times he caught me stealing glances at him, other times I saw him unabashedly admiring me from afar.

I had almost convinced myself that Krish was merely my director, and any thoughts beyond that were just distractions. Yet, the unspoken chemistry between us simmered beneath the surface, adding an electrifying touch to all our encounters. We didn't get an opportunity to speak to each other again in private, but yes, he was very much around in the facility, making me all the more aware of his every action.

The routine continued until today when I emerged from my shower, and a message from my team illuminated my phone screen, spelling out my first mission. The thrill of anticipation coursed through my veins as I read the instructions—Blue Moon Café, Table number 7, a man in a navy blue cap. He's our suspect attempting to smuggle diamonds, and my task was to just keep an eye on him until Team Beta took over and arrested both him and the other party with whom he was going to smuggle those diamonds.

Excitement surged through me. Finally, a mission to call my own. Though seemingly straightforward, I knew that simplicity could often be deceptive in a world where danger lurked behind every corner. Still, the prospect of actively contributing to GLEN's endeavours fuelled my anticipation.

I suited up and left my room with a sense of purpose. For now, the thoughts of Krish's charm and the powerful magnetism would have to take a back seat. With each step towards the café, I rehearsed the plan in my mind, ready to keep my eyes and ears open and be a silent observer. The described suspect, a man sporting a navy blue cap, was seated at Table number 7, his gaze scrutinising everyone entering.

Maintaining an air of nonchalance, I looked for a seat that would give me a clear view of him, but my hopes were dashed as the café was brimming with patrons, except for a man sitting alone at a table of two, engrossed in a newspaper. As he lowered the paper, my jaw dropped—it was Krish.

I approached Krish's table with a mix of shock and disbelief. "What are you doing here?" I questioned, leaning down and placing my hands firmly on the table—my expression a blend of surprise and irritation.

"Hey," Krish greeted me with a dazzling smile that sent a strange flutter through my stomach.

"I asked you something," I persisted, poking him lightly.

Krish lifted his mug, took a sip of his coffee, and then licked his lower lip before responding. "Well, I asked someone for a coffee date, but that person denied it, so I thought of pampering myself and go on a date alone. Do you have a problem with that?" he teased.

I gently banged my palms on the table before taking a seat beside him. To any onlookers, we might have seemed like a couple on a casual coffee date.

"Why are you always around whenever I am chasing my suspects?" I asked, furrowing my brow.

"Suspects?" Krish glanced around. "Don't tell me we need to fight a group of assailants here too, Trisha. In fact, I should ask you, why are you always ruining my 'ME' time? First in the men's washroom and now here when I am enjoying my strong coffee?" he continued with a playful grin, deliberately poking fun at me.

"Fine, enjoy your coffee date... ALONE," I retorted, ready to leave. However, Krish surprised me by grabbing my hand and compelling me to sit again next to him. "Don't go," he said, his words unexpectedly making my heart flutter. Even Krish seemed taken aback by the emotion in his own statement. Then he cleared his throat before adding, "I mean, if you are here to keep an eye on your suspect, this is the best spot."

I looked at him, a bit stunned. "You know about my mission tonight?"

"Being one of the directors of the organisation you work for, you think that was difficult for me?" Krish nonchalantly shrugged.

I glanced at Table number 7 again to ensure the suspect was still there.

"Are you stalking me now, Krish?" I really wanted to know and he didn't disappointment me.

"Maybe," he responded coyly, leaving me momentarily speechless.

I looked away, unable to decide how to take this conversation further.

Krish was openly admitting that he was tailing me. What was that supposed to mean? As I continued to stare at Table number 7, I heard Krish tapping his finger on the table to get my attention.

"If you stare at him so openly, he'll figure out in no time that you are here to catch him," he warned.

I turned back to Krish, trying to keep my focus split between him and the suspect.

"I know. I am not making it that obvious," I countered defensively.

To distract myself, I picked up Krish's mug and took a sip of his coffee. In a split second, I realised my slip-up and put the mug down. But it was too late. Krish already had a mischievous grin on his lips.

"Woah! Didn't see that coming," he teased. "I'm glad our coffee 'date' is coming true, though you're more fixated on the suspect rather than the man whose coffee you are sipping."

He never could stop flirting, could he?

"I have never seen a boss who distracts his own agent from focusing on her mission," I retorted, giving him a scolding look.

Krish leaned back, crossing his arms in front of him.

"This is the second time you are mentioning that I make you lose your focus, Trisha... Does that mean something?"

I didn't know what it meant, but with Krish around, I did tend to lose my focus, even if it was for a fraction of a second. Unsure of how to respond, I avoided meeting his eye again and shifted my attention to Table number 6 instead. A handsome man was sitting there, texting on his phone. Something about him seemed off, but I couldn't quite put my finger on it. It was like he was pretending to be cool.

Soon, my gaze returned to Table number 7, and that's when a tall man entered the café. He glanced at Table number 7 and swiftly walked over. He had a look of a criminal, making me instantly alert. Working against crime for years, I had developed a keen ability for identifying suspicious behaviour, intuitively reading their intentions from subtle cues. This man and the one at Table number 7 didn't give me good vibes.

"It must be him," Krish alerted me too.

I nodded gently, my eyes returning to the door, which opened again, and a woman entered, happily running to the guy at Table number 6. They exchanged a quick kiss before sitting down.

"Looks like the deal is going to happen any moment now," Krish murmured, and I was instantly attentive to every detail at Table number 7. However, my focus shifted occasionally to Table number 6, where the couple was now holding hands. The way their fingers intertwined seemed peculiar, raising my suspicion.

"You look more interested in the lovebirds than the suspects," Krish interrupted. "I think them holding hands, exchanging kisses... is distracting you."

I shot him a deadpan look.

"This is not the time for your jokes, Krish. Let me focus."

He chuckled softly, acknowledging the gravity of the situation. As the tension in the air escalated, I noticed from the window that Team Beta had arrived, and were disembarking from a speeding van and waiting for the right moment to intervene. The man with the navy blue cap at Table number 7 retrieved something from his pocket and handed it to the menacing-looking man who had recently joined him.

"Hands up!" Team Beta shouted, intervening at that very moment to arrest them both. Guns were aimed at the suspects seated at Table number 7, sending shockwaves through the other customers in the café.

"Everyone else, out…" the head of Team Beta ordered, instructing civilians to leave the premises. As the chaos unfolded, I stepped forward, taking out my gun and aiming it at the couple from Table number 6, who were preparing to leave with the rest of the crowd.

"Trisha? What are you doing? Why have you aimed the gun at these innocent civilians?" the head of Team Beta shouted at me, his confusion evident.

"They are the real suspects, not the ones at Table number 7," I replied firmly. Ignoring their curious gazes, I proceeded to frisk the woman at Table number 6 thoroughly. To everyone's surprise, I uncovered a stash of diamonds concealed in the inner pocket of her denim jacket.

Team Beta's leader looked stunned as I handed him the diamonds. Simultaneously, his team frisked the two men at Table number 7, finding nothing. I had been right.

"How?" Team Beta's head asked, his disbelief evident.

"I sensed something was amiss the moment I arrived here," I remarked. "The way this couple was tightly holding hands suggested an exchange was taking place. Their expressions, eye contact, and the winning smirk on their faces as they openly smuggled diamonds in the midst of this crowd — pretending to be an ordinary couple — did not escape my notice. That's how I identified them as the suspects, not the men at Table number 7. Although the latter initially appeared suspicious, their expressions and behaviour didn't match those of true criminals."

As soon as the words left my lips, a round of applause erupted behind me. Krish was clapping, clearly proud of my insight. Soon, everyone in the café, including the fake suspects at Table number 7 and the couple from Table number 6 from whom we recovered the diamonds, joined in the applause. Even the Beta Team members, who had initially aimed their weapons, now lowered them with smiles on their faces.

Hold on a second! What was happening?

Krish walked over, a smirk playing on his lips. "Well done, Agent Trisha. You never fail to surprise. Always one step ahead. You have cleared the mock mission test with flying colours."

Mock mission test? All this was to test my intellect? It wasn't real?

"Was this all a setup?" I questioned him, and he nodded his head, signalling the team to wrap up. The members began dispersing.

"Yes, it's a procedure—the final stage of your training to be part of the active missions. You didn't just blindly follow the details of the mission provided to you; instead, you correctly apprehended the real culprits," he explained.

I sighed. A part of me felt pleased that, even unknowingly, I had successfully cleared the test.

"It's all part of the job," he continued. "Observing the details, being vigilant and trusting your instincts. Plus, a bit of unpredictability adds flair to the mission, isn't it? But despite all the distractions, you handled it beautifully."

I couldn't help but crack a smile.

"And what was your role in all this?" I inquired. "I'm sure the Director doesn't have that much time to be a part of every trainee's mock mission test like today's."

Krish's lips curved into another smile before he stepped toward me, almost invading my private space. Our eyes locked in an intense battle.

"You are not *just* one of the trainees for me," he replied without breaking our gazes. "You will always be special, Trisha."

My heart fluttered at his choice of words. *Special?* What did he mean? Before I could process my thoughts, Krish winked at me and walked away. Fortunately, I had the table behind me to lean on because I needed its support badly. Krish's wink had the power to topple me off the floor, and I definitely liked myself more—a lot more than I liked him.

CHAPTER 3 (WAR OF HEARTS)

KRISH

I was at the combat training room early on a Sunday, working out my frustrations on the punching bag. This morning, my dad, who happened to be the president of GLEN, called me, questioning why I hadn't returned to Austria yet and what was prolonging my stay in India. Even though all the necessary paperwork was completed, I couldn't bring myself to explain that taking the next flight back would mean putting miles between me and the woman who had been occupying my thoughts—Trisha. Ever since meeting Trisha, I hadn't been able to get her out of my head. These days, I often thought about her strength, skill, and undeniable beauty. She was unlike any woman I had ever met. Despite the training protocols at GLEN, emphasizing the need to keep personal lives separate from missions, even if it meant giving them up, I couldn't seem to stop thinking about her. I felt an undeniable desire to get to know Trisha better, to spend time with her. Although I already knew every detail of her personal life through the background check conducted when we hired her, I found myself craving more.

With each punch, I replayed the puzzled expression on my dad's face during our video call earlier today when I informed him about needing an extra week or two in India to wrap up some undisclosed matters. I could have come up with a more convincing excuse, but at that moment, nothing came to mind. Dad's reaction made it clear that he wasn't buying my explanation either. He possessed the ability to see though my lies just by looking at me, a skill he excelled at. It wasn't just limited to me; his adeptness at psychologically reading any agent made it nearly impossible to keep secrets from him. There was a reason he held the position of President in this international law enforcement organisation—decades of experience and unparalleled knowledge had honed his ability to understand the minds and struggles of individuals.

I was lost in thought when suddenly I heard her voice behind me. "I didn't know Directors had to keep up with the combat training," Trisha said playfully.

I glanced back, my heart leaping at the sight of her. Hoping to sound casual, I replied with a flirtatious wink, "Not all Directors. Only those aiming to impress certain agents."

I felt her cheeks flush, but she tried to remain nonchalant. I continued to punch the bag while she watched me admiringly as I showed off my moves. I was eager to impress her, and landed my hardest punches.

"It's been a while since I practiced this," I admitted as I continued.

"Here, let me." She stepped forward to hold the bag steady for me. Thrilled by her proximity, I resumed my rhythmic punches as she observed closely.

"Your form is good, but you're dropping your left shoulder on those crosses," she said. "To maximise the effectiveness and power of each punch, you need to correct that form."

Unable to resist demonstrating, Trisha gently placed a hand on my shoulder. "Keep it up, like this."

Her touch ignited sparks within me, and I couldn't help but steal glances at her lovely face as she corrected my posture.

"Yes, that's it," she added, providing guidance while catching glimpses of my charming smile, reserved only for her. We both were hyper-aware of our closeness, our hands occasionally brushing against each other. By the end, all I wanted was to keep her by my side.

Grabbing a towel, I kept my gaze fixed on her.

"We should train together more often," I suggested, my voice unintentionally soft. "At least until I am here."

My heart soared as she warmly smiled. This woman had awakened something in me that I had never felt before.

"And how long are you here?" Trisha inquired.

"Two more weeks," I shrugged. "So, let's make the most of it."

"Are you inviting me on a combat training date, Director?" she smiled again, making my heart flutter even more.

"Why not? But if you don't like it, maybe we can settle for a real date… over dinner?" I suggested hopefully.

I really longed to know her better beyond our physical chemistry during training.

"We'll see, Director," she replied, letting the possibility linger tantalisingly between us.

Trisha then turned to leave, unable to hide her own smile. Watching her walk away, I knew I had to find out if what we had between us was more than just attraction. Being with Trisha made me believe that maybe, just maybe, I could experience a feeling deeper than anything I'd ever known—Love.

****

<u>A week later</u>

Since that day, Trisha and I continued to cross paths during her morning workout in the gym or in the combat training room, where I practiced my combat skills. We slowly fell into easy conversation, chatting and joking about nothing of significance. With Trisha, things just felt natural and unforced. Time seemed to stand still during those perfect moments when it was just the two of us, all professional barriers forgotten.

I found myself sharing things with her that I normally kept private. I shared about my life as a Director at GLEN in Austria, the encouragement and trust I received from my father, and my close-knit circle of friends. About Ayaan Shergill, my best friend and fellow Director at GLEN in Austria, who held a special place in my life. I told her almost everything. Trisha was so easy to talk to, and she always listened with genuine interest. In return, I was fascinated by learning tidbits about her life outside of GLEN. Every new detail, no matter how small, felt like discovering a hidden treasure. She was slowly opening up to me like I was happily bonding with her.

It was a quiet Sunday morning, and I was in my office finishing up some reports that just couldn't wait. As the Director of GLEN, the concept of a "day off" didn't really exist for me. I was so focused on the task at hand that I didn't even hear the knock at my door at first. When I glanced up, I was pleasantly surprised to see Trisha entering my office holding two steaming cups of coffee.

"Thought you could use a pick-me-up," she said with a smile, offering me one of the cups.

"You read my mind," I replied gratefully as I accepted the coffee. A faint electric spark surged through me as our fingers lightly brushed during the exchange. However, my attention shifted to her ring finger, adorned with a thin gold band. Discomfort settled within me at the thought of Trisha being engaged again. I knew she had a broken engagement in the past. Had they reconciled?

"Beautiful, isn't it?" she remarked, noticing my gaze on her ring finger.

I nodded absentmindedly, hesitant to inquire about the ring but also not wanting to reveal my evident disapproval of her engagement, if it were true.

"I never noticed this on your finger before," I mentioned, clearing my throat.

"I rarely wear it. We're not allowed such accessories at work. But today is special, so I decided to put it on. I hope you don't mind," she explained.

I do mind if that is your engagement ring — my subconscious protested. But I held back from voicing my suspicions to Trisha.

"And what's so special today?" I broached the subject again as I watched Trisha making herself comfortable, perching on the edge of my desk like she belonged there.

Seeing her dressed so casually in a t-shirt and jeans was a refreshing change from her usual tactical gear. She looked beautiful, bathed in the morning sunlight streaming through my window.

"It's my Mumma's birthday today," she responded with a smile. "This is her ring; she gave it to me before she passed away a few years ago. I wear it every year on this day to honour her memory."

"Your mother's ring?" I clarified, exhaling in relief.

"Yes, my mother's ring. What did you think?" she asked, and I shook my head, avoiding any indication of my earlier suspicions.

"Nothing," I replied, sipping the coffee and smiling in relief before placing the mug on the table.

"So tell me, Mr. Director, don't you ever take a day off?" Trisha asked, her playful tone seemingly aware of my discomfort, possibly thinking the ring meant an engagement.

I gazed up at her, smitten. "I do take days off, albeit not regularly. However, today, I had a hunch that a stunning woman I admire would drop by my office, bringing specially brewed coffee and a smile to brighten my day," I flirted in response.

"Stop it." She laughed and nudged my shoulder lightly. The sound of her laughter was music to my ears.

There was a ping on her phone, and as she read the message, I knew our impromptu coffee break was over. *Too soon!*

"Got to go. We have some intel on the drug lord we are looking for. Need to work on that," Trisha conveyed, rising from the desk and heading towards the door. A pang of disappointment hit me; I wasn't ready for this stolen moment of closeness to end.

Just as she reached the door, Trisha glanced back with a playful glint in her eyes. "You know where to find me if you need more coffee," she said sincerely, raising her mug.

"What if I don't need more coffee but good company to hear the story behind that ring and your mother? The dinner date offer is still open," I teased.

She bit her lip, slightly flustered, and rolled her eyes before making her exit. I couldn't keep the grin off my face as I watched her disappear out the door. Even after she was gone, I found myself replaying every second we had shared, marvelling at how Trisha had the power to make even the most mundane day feel extraordinary. If this was just a small taste of what it could be like between us, then I was excited to see where this undeniable connection might lead next. Trisha had awakened a longing in my heart I never knew existed.

TRISHA

With each passing day, I found myself more drawn towards Krish despite my attempts to remain professional. There was so much about this man that drew me in and excited me. He had awakened in me hopes and emotions I'd long kept dormant. In my life, I'd always prioritised my career over relationships. Even with Sanjay, my ex-fiancée, it was never like this. There were no secret glances, playful banter, or electrifying touches. But with Krish, every interaction left me yearning for more.

As a GLEN agent, I knew I should keep my distance. Personal ties were dangerous in this world of covert missions. But when Krish was near, my professional instincts faltered. Being around him awakened my feminine side that craved affection. *His affection.*

Our recent lighthearted moments together had shown me a glimpse of something beautiful developing between us. He had a way of making me feel special in a way no one else ever had. And in his absence, I kept replaying his flirtatious words and stolen glances in my mind.

I had no doubt Krish, too, felt this undeniable connection between us. His heart also fluttered every time our hands accidentally touched. With Krish, I felt a sense of possibility that both thrilled and terrified me. I knew giving in to my feelings was risky. Yet the thought of denying this rare chance at love pained me too. For now, I could only take each moment as it came, while my heart continued to wish for more.

I was in the intelligence room, focusing on the case files for an upcoming mission, when Krish walked in. And as usual, whenever he was around, I found it hard to focus anywhere else.

"Hey there," Krish greeted casually, pulling up a chair beside me. "Prepping for the Drug Lord case?"

I nodded, trying to remain professional even as my pulse quickened being so close to him.

"I was thinking..." Krish continued, his tone thoughtful. "For a case this big, we should celebrate after cracking it. Maybe over dinner?" His gaze held a tentative hopefulness.

"Why are you so fixated on the dinner thing?" I inquired, locking eyes with him.

"Wrong question," he smirked, leaning in closer. "I'm not fixated on just the dinner thing, but a date with you, over dinner." Krish winked at me before adding, "I've even decided what I'm going to wear for our dinner date. How about Bermuda shorts, a linen button-up shirt, flip flops, and a straw hat? Does that tempt you?"

Gosh, he never missed a chance to flirt.

"Are we heading to a beach location for dinner?"

"That sounds like fun, doesn't it? I love beaches. What about you? Are you a beach person or do you prefer hill stations?"

Unsure how to respond, I lightly bumped his shoulder with mine. "Neither. And cracking the case comes first, Director," I replied in a playfully evasive tone.

Krish sighed.

"You're right, duty calls." He was about to get up but then paused, his gaze danced mischievously as he looked at me again. "But just so you know, I don't give up so easily on things I really want."

My cheeks flushed at the insinuation. Our gaze lingered longer than needed. This was the first time I caught a whiff of his aftershave, or was it his musky, woodsy cologne?

"Just a dinner date, Agent Trisha," he insisted. "I have only two days here before I fly back to Austria."

His eyes pleaded with me to say yes, and then he left. I watched him saunter away, while trying to keep my heart in check. Despite my better instincts, I was looking forward to what might unfold next. Would I continue to decline his request for a dinner date, or would he succeed in convincing me?

The Next Morning...

Krish was in the middle of his morning workout routine at the GLEN gym facility. Clad in a sleeveless vest that highlighted his muscular arms and track pants, he was engrossed in a set of pushups. As he rhythmically lowered and raised his body, a light sheen of sweat glistened on his skin.

Unbeknownst to him, I walked into the gym at that very moment and paused in my tracks, momentarily distracted by the sight of Krish's athletic form. His focused expression as he trained, the flex of his arm muscles with each pushup—it all made my heart involuntarily flutter.

"Is that an expression of admiration on your face?" Krish inquired, glancing at me and breaking into a grin.

"83...84...85," he counted his pushups aloud in his breathy voice.

"You observe too much," I muttered, moving further ahead.

"Do I?" he chuckled. "Then why are you here? To join me for a workout, Agent Trisha?" he asked with a playful glint in his eyes.

"Perhaps," I replied coyly.

"Quit giving me evasive answers. I know you're mesmerised watching me do the pushups."

I laughed. "Oh, please, Director. I've seen agents doing pushups with weights on their backs. That's the kind of scene that captures my attention. What you're doing is just the basics."

Krish stopped doing the pushups.

"You are talking to the Director, Agent. I've done more than just basics. Don't underestimate me. Back in Austria, during my training,

I've shouldered more weight during pushups than you can ever imagine."

"Really?" I asked, walking over, and before Krish could react, I sat lightly on his back as he remained in his pushup position.

"Is 55 kg enough of a challenge for you to do ten more pushups like this, Director?" I dared.

Krish chuckled at my bold move, a thrill sparking in his eyes, visible in the large wall mirror before us. "Or is that all you've got?"

I crossed my legs and perched on his back, applying my full weight. To my surprise, Krish continued with his pushups. Honestly, I didn't expect him to. I'd settled on his back, contributing just sufficient weight to transform his workout into a playful challenge. On the tenth pushup, Krish pretended to buckle under my weight, collapsing dramatically to the floor. I yelped in surprise as I fell with him, landing on his chest as he rolled over. We both continued to laugh until I realised that he had stopped laughing. Krish's eyes flitted to my lips, his heart racing at our sudden closeness. For a fleeting moment, our faces were inches apart, and the air between us crackled with possibility. Just as I was about to close my eyes, giving in to the unknown, the distinct sound of footsteps reached us from the gym door. And just like that, our spell was broken. We had been caught in that compromising position, in the vicinity of GLEN's building, by none other than the President of this organisation—Mr. Ratan Rajvanshi—Krish's father.

I scrambled to my feet, mildly flustered, while Krish helped himself up.

"Dad?" he uttered, a hint of surprise in his voice. "What... what are you doing here?"

"Director," his father responded strictly. "In my cabin, now," he commanded, casting me a disapproving glance before leaving the scene.

Shit! My eyes met with Krish's in a wordless exchange before I left the gym, grappling with the realisation that I might have just jeopardised our professional standing.

CHAPTER 4
(CROSSROADS)
KRISH

Dad had seen me with Trisha in the gym and summoned me to his cabin. He didn't look pleased, which I understood because he didn't like anyone in GLEN breaking the protocols that Trisha and I had done today. *Almost.* I followed Dad into his office cabin, irritated by the fact that he had directed his assistant to summon Trisha as well. I wasn't happy with this development since I knew Dad wouldn't be lenient on Trisha, which I didn't want.

As soon as we entered the room and the door closed behind us, I asked indignantly, "Dad? What are you doing here?"

He whirled around furiously and snapped, "What are *you* doing here, Krish? What do you think you're doing fooling around with Agent Trisha?"

I sensed the accusatory tone in his voice.

"We were not fooling around! Whatever you think you saw doesn't matter. Our relationship is strictly professional," I replied, keeping my tone in check.

"Don't you dare lie to me, Krish! I know exactly what I saw between the two of you. You were blatantly flirting and letting your personal feelings get in the way of your work and judgement," he accused.

"Trisha is a friend, Dad. She is one of the best agents we've recruited recently—"

"I know everything about Trisha. I don't need you to fill me in," he snapped. "How could you, out of all, allow whatever happened back there to happen? You two may be friends, but what I just witnessed as the President of GLEN was not appropriate."

"I know the timing was not ideal but I assure you whatever you saw will never come in between our work. Our personal lives have nothing to do with Trisha and my professional responsibilities."

"Whatever was going on between the two of you was not right for either of you professionally, and I can say that as both the head of this organisation and as your father."

"What's not right about it?" I kept arguing, annoyed at his accusations.

Dad looked exasperated. "I can't believe I have to spell this out for you, but if you need to hear it from me, here it is. You know very well that agents getting romantically involved with each other is strictly against our rules. Your sole focus should be on the missions you are working on, not on impressing each other."

I was irritated at his choice of words.

"We are not neglecting our missions. Trisha is working hard to find the drug cartel we've been chasing for years. In fact, the intel and insights she has provided have been crucial in our investigation."

Dad still seemed unconvinced. "She may be contributing to the missions, but I can clearly see she is losing focus now. All her attention seems to be on you, not the tasks at hand."

"You're completely misinterpreting this," I shot back.

Dad looked even more furious.

"I'm misinterpreting? Really, Krish? You were supposed to finish the paperwork here and return to Austria last week, but you didn't. You gave me excuses about other unfinished work that I wasn't aware of. Was this your real reason for extending your stay? To spend more time with Trisha?" Dad's voice held a mix of disappointment and frustration.

I struggled to come up with a response, realising my father had seen through my ruse.

"Alright. Yes, I extended my stay here because I wanted to spend time with Trisha," I admitted with a firm resolve. "I like her, Dad. And I kept it from you because I knew you would be reacting exactly the way you are reacting now."

His expression hardened.

"If you cared about her that much, Krish, you shouldn't have involved her with GLEN. You could've pursued something outside the organisation and spared her from these complications. But since she's part of GLEN now, let her focus on the missions."

I was rendered speechless, unable to counter his argument. There was a truth in his words that I couldn't deny. Dad maintained a stern gaze, continuing his admonition, "I don't want Trisha repeating the same mistake she made in RAW, where personal feelings compromised her professional commitment. I won't tolerate any slip-ups from her."

Confusion clouded my mind. "What mistake? She was fired from RAW for killing the target instead of arresting him."

His sigh was heavy. "Is that all you found in your background check, Krish? Trisha did kill the target, deviating from her orders, but it was to save her fiancé."

Saving her fiancé? I knew about Trisha's broken engagement after leaving RAW, but I didn't know the details.

"She killed the target to save her fiancé's life," Dad continued. "She chose her personal relationship over her duty and compromised an important mission. That's why she was dismissed from her previous role."

I struggled to process this new information. I had recruited Trisha, believing her skills made her an invaluable asset to GLEN, despite knowing about her failure in RAW. And even now, Dad's words didn't change my belief in her. I was aware of her capabilities. As someone who admired her, I understood her decision to prioritise her fiancé's life over her professional duties. However, as the Director of GLEN, I couldn't condone my agents failing in their responsibilities due to personal reasons.

"She let her personal ties interfere with her duty, and that's why she was fired from her role. If you and Trisha get involved personally, and she prioritises you over missions, I won't stand for it. I won't accept failures in GLEN, Krish. Do you want to be the reason behind her downfall this time?"

Just then, I heard a small gasp behind me. Dad shifted his gaze behind me, and his expression grew colder. I turned to see Trisha standing hesitantly at the door. She had been summoned here as well and had likely overheard the entire conversation.

Her face mirrored the hurt and conflict I felt inside me. Dad directed a sharp question at her, "Do you have anything to say for yourself, Agent?"

Trisha's attempt to respond was met with a heavy silence. She looked apologetic and hurt.

"I'm sorry, Sir. I wouldn't let any failures reflect on GLEN on my account ever. I promise until I am a part of GLEN, I won't give you any reason to doubt my dedication and commitment to this organisation again. I am truly sorry."

She turned and hurriedly left before I could say anything. I felt awful seeing her so upset. Dad's words replayed in my mind. Despite the validity of his points, I wasn't pleased with the way everything unfolded in front of him. Trisha and I hadn't even begun to openly acknowledge our feelings, and now, it seemed like she would distance herself from me. The thought stung. If we pursued a relationship, it could risk everything we had worked for, yet I wanted her.

I remained lost in my thoughts when Dad's hand landed on my shoulder, bringing me back to the present.

"Krish, up until now, I was warning you as the President of GLEN. But now, as your father, I want to tell you this. I can see it in your eyes — you care for Trisha deeply. In all these years, I've never seen you so taken with any woman. I can sense a special connection between you two. If you truly want to pursue something with her in the future, here's my advice."

He paused, choosing his words with a paternal care that touched me deeply.

"Now you know the real reason why Trisha was fired from RAW. But she's skilled and passionate about her work — I recognise that. Let her prove herself in this role. Give her the time to showcase her capabilities and professionalism. She's just completed her training and is handling critical missions. Allow her to prove herself through her work. Then, you can decide how you both want to proceed. I won't stand in your way. If Trisha becomes a part of our family in the future, I would be more than happy. I trust your judgement. Whoever you choose will be the best for you and our family. But for now, let her prove herself on the professional front."

Despite the logic in his advice, the reality of drawing a line between personal and professional felt daunting. I fought back tears, overwhelmed by the gravity of this situation.

"Just as you're passionate about GLEN and handling your role as Director, I believe Trisha is equally committed to her responsibilities in this organisation. I don't want her to regret getting personally involved with you, neglecting her professional duties, and later blaming you for any repercussions."

His words struck a chord within me. While I wanted to support Trisha's professional growth, the challenge of maintaining a professional boundary seemed daunting. But at that moment, my immediate concern was checking on Trisha, ensuring that the events of the day hadn't left her upset or angry with me.

TRISHA

I hurried out of the president's office, blinking back furious tears. How could I have been so stupid to let my guard down with Krish? I should have known better than to jeopardise my career again over personal feelings.

Returning to the training centre, I grabbed a noise-cancelling headset and a gun, taking aim at the human-shaped target board ahead. With each shot that landed squarely on the target's head, I was transported back to that fateful mission a year ago.

Working for RAW, I had been tasked with catching a dangerous arms smuggler alive. The mission took an unexpected turn when my fiancé, Sanjay, joined me in this operation. Sanjay, a decent man and a friend of my cousin brother, shared the same dreams and aspirations as I did—to contribute something significant to our country.

At that time, my grandmother, who was around 90 years old, was unwell, and her last wish was to see me settled in life. Despite my initial reluctance towards the idea of marriage, I agreed when my cousin brother Ravi brought the proposal of Sanjay. Knowing Sanjay from before and acknowledging the practicality of having a life partner with similar professional goals, I agreed to the engagement. It was a conventional arrangement, devoid of any overwhelming emotions on my part.

Within two months of the engagement, the cracks began to appear. Sanjay's family started pressuring me to quit my job after marriage. Our disagreements on this matter were frequent, and Sanjay seemed incapable of taking a stand or asserting his side. The tension escalated when a mission came our way—an apparently straightforward task. We received intel that the arms smuggler was holed up in a deserted factory with a handful of men. Our sole objective was to capture him alive.

As we approached the factory site, little did I know that this mission would become a turning point in my life, testing the delicate balance between personal relationships and professional obligations.

I crept along the crumbling wall of the abandoned factory, my senses on high alert. Sanjay was somewhere on the opposite side, preparing to ambush the arms smuggler and his men once I gave the signal. No matter how simple the task looked, my heart still pounded with exhilaration and fear.

As I peered around the corner, I spotted my target. He was a tall, imposing figure, barking orders at his lackeys as they loaded wooden crates onto a truck. No doubt, it was full of illegal weapons and ammunition. I steadied my nerves and waited for the right moment.

Suddenly, a shout went up from one of the lookouts. We had been spotted! Without hesitation, I burst from my hiding place, gun drawn.

"Freeze! Hands in the air!"

The smugglers scrambled for their weapons, and from nowhere, more bullets were fired at us. Everything happened so fast. One moment, Sanjay and I were closing in on the arms smuggler. The next, all hell broke loose. Gunfire erupted from all directions as the smugglers realised they were surrounded. Sanjay and I dove for cover, shots whizzing past us. We returned fire, but they had us pinned down.

Our target tried to flee the chaotic scene. This was our chance — if he got away, the mission would be a failure. I broke cover, racing after him. Sanjay also chased that smuggler, but in just a fraction of a second, I heard Sanjay cry out in pain. He fell to the ground, blood spreading across his thigh from a gunshot wound. Our target — the arms smuggler, stood over him, ready to fire the kill shot.

In that split second, my heart dropped. I had an impossible choice — pursue the target as ordered and arrest him alive, or kill him and save Sanjay's life. Orders or love. Duty or family. My mind raced. Sanjay's eyes met mine, wide with fear and pain. And in that moment, I knew what I had to do. I aimed and fired two quick shots, taking down the arms smuggler who was about to kill Sanjay.

Though we had taken down all of the men here and stopped the smuggling, the mission failed terribly as I had shot down the target and disobeyed my given orders.

RAW dismissed me swiftly after that mission failure. I couldn't forget the anger and disappointment on my senior officer's face.

"You allowed your personal life to compromise an important mission,

Agent Trisha!" he had shouted. "This is unacceptable. You are fired."

At the time, I had been defiant, insisting I would choose Sanjay over any mission. Only later did the full weight of my actions sink in. I had sacrificed everything for one person. My career, my reputation, my sense of self-worth — all gone in an instant. And the worst was yet to come. Sanjay's revelation later shattered the fragile balance between my personal and professional life. He informed me that he had chosen to side with his family, supporting their demand for me to quit my career after RAW terminated my services. He envisioned a future where I would solely focus on our impending marriage, taking on the role of his housewife. The weight of his expectations pressed on me, threatening to drown my ambitions.

In a heated confrontation, I reached my breaking point. Pulling off the engagement ring, I hurled it at him, vehemently expressing my frustration.

"I chose you over my mission and career, Sanjay. Yet, it seems you fail to understand the sacrifice I made. Despite being in a position to contribute significantly to our country, you deny equal rights to women with similar aspirations. I refuse to be associated with a man like you."

With those words, I closed the chapter of that relationship, vowing to leave it behind forever.

It took me a few months to heal from the emotional wounds. However, I didn't let this setback affect my commitment to serving the country. I redirected my efforts to the state police department, moving on from that turbulent chapter of my life.

Today's argument between Krish and his father brought back the shadows of judgment stemming from my past failures. Their words, though unspoken by Krish, echoed the doubt that lingered in the air. It was a reminder that people still measured me by the choices I had made. Krish might be a good man, but the fear of history repeating itself gnawed at me. I couldn't afford to fall for someone who might judge me based on my past.

I couldn't risk another disastrous relationship with a man who might question my dedication to my duty. Krish deserved someone who could reciprocate his feelings fully, unburdened by the shadows of past choices.

Taking a deep, shaky breath, I resolved not to let that happen. I could not — would not — make the same mistake twice. I had promised GLEN my full dedication, and I intended to uphold it, no matter what it cost me personally. As I mechanically loaded and fired my gun again, I hardened my heart and shut out any thought of Krish. I was an agent of GLEN now, nothing more.

CHAPTER 5 (GONE WITH THE WIND)

KRISH

The clouds drifted by my window, but I hardly noticed them. My mind was still back in that office, replaying the conversation with my father over and over.

"Don't get too attached, Krish. This is a professional relationship, nothing more," he had warned about Trisha. "She failed her last mission by choosing personal feelings over duty. Don't make her repeat the same mistake."

His words echoed in my head, mingling with the pounding ache in my chest. He was right, of course. Trisha and I were colleagues. Whatever magnetic pull I felt towards her, I had to ignore it.

But it wasn't that simple. Somewhere along the way, she had become more than just the woman who worked in my organisation. I yearned to see her smile and to hear her laugh. I lived for our conversations, both serious and playful. She challenged me, supported me, and I was different with her altogether.

When she looked at me, it felt like... like maybe she felt the same way. That there was a connection between us, we couldn't deny.

Was I fooling myself? Had I misunderstood her closeness? Had I interpreted her warmth as something more?

Maybe. But now, I would never know.

As soon as she got my father's warning, Trisha pulled away. That very night, she left for Malaysia, halfway across the world from me, chasing a lead for her drug cartel's case. But we both knew the truth. She was putting distance between us on purpose. After what my father said, she saw the risk in getting closer and made the choice to retreat back to business. And just like that, the spell was broken.

Now, here I sat on this plane, staring blankly out the window, sipping the champagne which turned bitter in my mouth. She slipped away before I could speak to her or even meet her eyes. And it ached — goddamn, it ached — like a hole in my chest.

But I had no right to feel hurt. Trisha did the responsible thing for both of us. She rededicated herself to the job, to GLEN, and I had to respect her decision, as much as it stung.

With a heavy sigh, I turned from the window. I couldn't change how she felt. All I could do was follow her lead and refocus on my role at work. That was the life we had chosen. Anything and everything else would have to wait.

<u>Six months Later</u>

Six months had passed since I'd seen or spoken to Trisha, since she flew off into the night, putting her mission first.

I returned to Austria, but I'd kept tabs on her from afar through my team. Her accomplishments were impressive — she'd gotten closer than anyone to unravelling the powerful drug cartel she'd been tracking ever since she joined GLEN.

But her methods made me uneasy. Going undercover, she had infiltrated the organisation by posing as the girlfriend of Max, the ringleader's younger brother. It was dangerous work, putting her at constant risk if her cover was blown.

And the longer she kept up with this act, the more inevitable it seemed that she would have to get... closer to Max. A nauseating but logical step to gain his trust and get information. The thought twisted my gut and filled me with frustration.

I knew it shouldn't matter. This was all part of the job. And Trisha was smart and capable of handling herself. Yet, it disturbed me. I couldn't get the image out of my head — her with him. Laughing at his jokes, letting him put his arm around her waist, kissing her. *My Trisha.*

No, not mine. I gave up that right long ago. I'd stayed away. I'd respected her space and her dedication to this mission above all else. Even if it had eaten me up inside these six months.

I kept picturing our last moment together. Her silhouette in the doorway, hesitating as if she might turn back. But she didn't. Trisha had just straightened her shoulders and walked away. Maybe by now, I was a distant memory for her. She'd moved on. She didn't even think of me anymore. After all, she'd been fully committed to bringing down this cartel, no matter the cost.

And here I was, thousands of miles away from her, unable to shake her from my mind. I checked for updates about her obsessively, hating this helplessness that I couldn't see her yet. There were times I really wished I could be there with her, watching her back and keeping her safe. But I gave up that thought, knowing Trisha needed to focus and deliver what she had chosen for herself — her first mission with GLEN. All I could do was wait and hope this mission ended soon, and that Trisha succeeded in her goals.

TRISHA

I spotted him across the crowded pub, just like the intel said he'd be. Max, the handsome younger brother of the drug cartel kingpin I was tracking. He was my way in.

I made sure he noticed me, too, throwing flirtatious glances his way while pretending to sip my drink. I'd been told Max had a thing for red hair and had to change the colour of my hair to successfully complete this mission. It worked. I stood out as the only woman with red hair, enough for him to notice me. When he finally approached and asked if the seat beside me was taken, I flashed him my most charming smile.

"It is now," I replied, giving him my most inviting smile.

We talked and laughed through the night, the alcohol lowering his defences. I steered the conversation, subtly pumping him for information while revealing just enough about myself to keep him intrigued.

By the end of the night, Max was smitten. But I left him wanting more, giving him only my first name and a fake number to remember me by. And that was enough.

Over the next weeks, I orchestrated more 'chance' encounters that were anything but. Every club, restaurant, and beach he visited, I'd be there, appearing out of the blue. Each time, the look in his eyes grew warmer.

He confessed it felt like fate, us meeting so often. It was just skillful manoeuvering on my part, carefully planned. But I smiled coyly, playing along like it was destiny. Each encounter brought new details about his brother's operation. But Max was impatient and tried to get physically closer. I would redirect him charmingly, not giving too much too soon. This was a delicate dance, gaining his trust while keeping him at arm's length. My gut churned with disgust at his touch and his hungry stares, but I had to sell this illusion.

Weeks turned into months. Max began to lower his guard, revealing key information he shouldn't have — the tiny flat they use for packaging drugs, the delivery route through the jungle, his brother's paranoia about being betrayed. He gave too much information, all so crucial for my team to catch his brother — the biggest drug cartel lord 'Ron'.

I stored away all that information, piecing together a map of their organisation. But keeping Max interested without taking things further was getting harder. The hunger in his eyes had intensified, and soon, he would demand more than just flirting and light caresses. I knew I was running out of time before I had to disappear. The thought of his hands on me made my skin crawl. Just a little longer, I always told myself. I was so close — just a little more and I'd have enough to bring his brother down.

****

<u>Present Day</u>

The music pulsed around me as I swayed half-heartedly on the dance floor. Max's hand gripped my waist possessively as we moved to the beat. I forced a smile, appearing to enjoy his attention. Inside, my thoughts drifted miles away… *To Krish.*

It still surprised me how often he crept into my mind lately. A wry comment that would make him chuckle. A beautiful sunset I wished I could share with him. The ache of missing someone after so long alone. Did he ever think of me? Or had he moved on and forgotten our brief connection considering the gravity of his job role as Director of GLEN?

I replayed our last moment together, when I'd overheard his father's warning. The awkward tension in the room. How I slipped away before Krish could stop me. My choice had felt so clear then — refocus on the work and don't get distracted. Be the agent I was trained to be. But part of me had hoped Krish might defy his father and come after me. Tell me we would figure things out together. Instead, he let me go without a fight. Maybe it was for the best. This life made relationships impossible. I was here, undercover, and Krish was a world away. Wanting anything more was dangerous and irresponsible.

Still, some nights, I would curl up alone and imagine his face and his smile, and the comfort I felt just being near him. A sense of peace

I had not known before or since enveloped me when I was with him. In the daylight, I buried those thoughts. But they would always return in the darkest hours, bittersweet reminders of what I could not have.

"You seem distracted tonight," Max muttered, pulling me closer with greedy hands. I tensed, then forced myself to relax into his embrace.

"Just tired," I lied with an apologetic smile. Over his shoulder, I saw one of his men approaching with some news. Back to work, back to the mission at hand.

My personal feelings would have to wait. I had a job to do. But that didn't stop my traitorous heart from whispering Krish's name, wondering where he was tonight under the same lonely moon.

I tensed as Max's men approached our table with urgent expressions on their faces. This was unusual—normally, any sensitive information was discussed freely in front of me. I was just Max's ditzy model girlfriend, totally harmless in their eyes.

But the way they glared at me now, full of suspicion... something was very wrong.

"We need to speak with you privately, boss," one of the henchmen muttered to Max under his breath. Max's expression darkened, but he nodded.

"I'll be right back, babe," he said casually to me, but his eyes were hard as steel. I sipped my drink slowly and nodded, watching them out of the corner of my eye.

They moved to a secluded corner, speaking in hushed, heated tones. Max's body language was rigid, his fists clenching at his sides. My pulse spiked with fear, but I kept my face neutral. As he listened to whatever news his men conveyed, his head whipped around to stare at me, pure hatred in his gaze.

My blood turned to ice as I watched Max and his men. Their heated whispers and furtive glances in my direction were enough to give me clues. *They knew.* Somehow, they had discovered my true identity. They knew I wasn't who I claimed to be, and it was evident in the barely contained rage I saw in Max's eyes.

I had to figure out what exactly they knew first. Buy time to assess the situation before they inevitably tried to take me out. My fingers tightened around my drink as I watched the tense conversation, barely breathing. Waiting for the axe to fall.

Max's hand slid inside his jacket, and I saw the unmistakable outline of a gun. He turned towards me with murder in his eyes. *Shit!* Time was running out. I had to act now. My mind raced through options, but I felt trapped. I was deep in their territory, outnumbered and outgunned. Max and his men could kill me in seconds if I made one wrong move.

In one smooth motion, I slipped my hand under my dress, clutching the gun strapped to my thigh. With a practiced motion, I drew it out. Screams erupted around me as people around saw my gun. Max whipped around at the sudden commotion, momentarily distracted. I took aim and fired a single shot into the ceiling. Chaos exploded. The crowd panicked, stampeding for the exits when they heard the gunshot. Using the confusion to my advantage, I flipped my table up, seeking cover behind it.

Max bellowed in rage, drawing out his weapon. Bullets peppered the table as I shielded myself behind it, feeling the wood splinter around me.

"I need cover," I screamed, speed dialling my team. "Code Red, I need backup now. Fast." I repeated before disconnecting the call.

I had to get out of here, fast. Crouching low, I crept along the perimeter of the room, firing shots to keep Max and his men at bay. I was almost to the fire exit when a bullet grazed my shoulder, but I gritted my teeth against the pain.

Get to the exit, Trisha. Get out. You can make it.

With a final sprint, I burst through the door, sirens already blaring in the distance. The mission was blown, but I was still breathing. Blood oozed from my shoulder, but I kept running. There was no going back now. All my months undercover, wasted in one moment. And after this, I knew Max would be after me relentlessly. As I disappeared into the dark city streets, my right arm throbbing, only one thought echoed in my mind. *Run.* Just run, and somehow make it out of here alive and reach the safe point where my team can pick me up.

My shoulder screamed in pain as I ran down the dark alleyway. With every step, I could feel more blood soaking my dress from the bullet's graze. But I couldn't stop.

Max and his men were close behind, their menacing threats echoing off the buildings. I had to make it to the rendezvous point where my extraction team would be waiting. My vision started to blur at the edges. How much further? I clung desperately to consciousness — passing out here would mean certain death.

Suddenly, a black van screeched around the corner ahead. Relief flooded through me. *My team.* With my last ounce of strength, I flagged them down. The van skidded to a stop, and strong arms pulled me inside, shutting out the pursuit and taking me to safety.

"Go, go, go!" came the urgent command as the van veered back into the street. Just then, bullets peppered the side of the vehicle — Max's men had caught up to us. I collapsed onto the van floor as my agents returned fire through the rear window. The pain in my shoulder made me flinch, but someone quickly applied pressure with bandages to my shoulder to stop the bleeding. We were speeding away from the danger now, but I was spent.

"Trisha, look at me! Stay with us!" My team leader shouted as everything started turning hazy, fading into nothingness. I had completed my mission and made it out alive, but only barely.

As I lost my grip on consciousness from the blood loss and sheer exhaustion, my last thoughts were of Krish. Would he hear what happened? Would I ever see him again...?

The world slipped away into darkness. But I had survived, and that was enough for now. Help had come, and I was safe.

CHAPTER 6 (GOT YOU)
TRISHA

I awoke with a gasp, my eyes flying open. For a moment, panic gripped me as I tried to get my bearings. The sterile white hospital room, the IV in my arm... then it came back in a rush. Max, the ambush, getting shot by his men at the club, and still alive.

As I struggled to sit up, the ache in my bandaged shoulder jolted me. I had survived, but only narrowly. Although the bullet that struck my shoulder hadn't penetrated the skin, the throbbing ache persisted. Touching the wound gingerly, I exhaled in relief. It could have been so much worse. I was lucky.

Reaching for the cup of water on the bedside table, I paused. There was a hand holding it out to me already. My eyes followed up the arm to the face I knew so well. *Krish.*

I froze, the cup halfway to my lips. What was he doing here? How did he even know what happened? Confusion swirled in my foggy brain.

"What are you doing here?" I asked hoarsely once I found my voice again.

Krish's expression was tight with emotion. "What do you think I'm doing here?"

My mind raced. Had he dropped everything and come when he heard I was shot? Despite me walking away from him without a word months ago? It made no sense.

"You shouldn't be here, Krish," I murmured. "Not after..." *Not after his father had forbidden us from getting close.* I completed that statement in my head instead of voicing it out. "You should leave."

Krish's jaw clenched at the unsaid reminder.

"I heard you didn't seem to want that when you were first brought in," he said quietly. "You kept saying my name repeatedly... even in your unconscious state."

I inhaled sharply. Even when barely conscious, some part of me had longed for Krish, needed him by my side. As much as I tried to deny it when awake, this was the truth. But I didn't want Krish to know that.

"Who… who told you that? The team? The doctors?" I asked in a panic.

I didn't want my colleagues to know that I harboured a soft spot for Krish. Honestly, I hadn't even admitted it to myself until now.

Seeing the conflict in my eyes, Krish sighed. "Drink some water first," he insisted.

I let him help me in holding the glass as I quickly drank the water. The next second, I coughed and sputtered as the water hit my parched throat. Krish was instantly at my side, stroking my back soothingly as I caught my breath.

"Easy," he murmured. His fingers lightly grazed my bare shoulder, and I shivered, the thin hospital gown leaving me exposed. Krish seemed oblivious, just focused on my coughing fit.

When I finally calmed down, he put the glass away with a look of relief.

"The team shouldn't know you're here," I said quickly, trying to steer the conversation away from dangerous waters.

"They know already." His expression darkened.

They know? What did they know?

"Your team knows I am here. They just don't know I'm here for personal reasons more than professional."

I swallowed nervously as Krish pulled a chair and sat next to my bed, leaning forward intently.

"Let's get to the main topic before we discuss the failed mission, Agent Trisha Choudhary."

For the first time, Krish addressed me by my last name. Unfortunately, the mission I had been dedicated to for the past few months with GLEN hadn't gone as planned. But it seemed like Krish had other personal matters to discuss before delving into the professional setbacks.

"You abandoned me, Trisha. The way you left, without a word… it tore me up."

"You know why I left," I argued. "We had an intel on Max and…"

"Was that the only reason you left?" he inquired.

I looked away, unable to respond.

"Look, Trisha, I respect your dedication to the work, I do. But I can't keep pretending there's nothing between us. No matter what my father demands."

He reached for my hand tentatively, but I pulled away.

"Your father didn't demand anything unreasonable, Krish. He just wanted us to draw boundaries, and as the president of GLEN, he has the authority to make such requests. We've committed ourselves, even our lives, to this organisation."

"I'm willing to sacrifice my life for GLEN, but they don't have the right to dictate when and to whom I give my heart."

His reply made my heart skip a beat.

"We need to discuss us, Trisha."

I looked away again, feigning confusion. "There is no 'us'."

"Don't," Krish said sharply. "You can lie to yourself but not to me. Even in this state, you were calling out for me, Trisha. Why?"

I paled, humiliation washing over me.

"That doesn't mean anything," I argued weakly. "I was not in the right mindset."

Krish grasped my hand firmly before I could pull away. "It means you still care, no matter how hard you pretend otherwise. I know you feel this too, Trisha."

Panic clawed at my throat. I couldn't let him break through my defences.

"What exactly is 'this' you're referring to?" I asked Krish pointedly. "Define it clearly because, as far as I'm concerned, love has no place in my life right now. Yes, I was engaged once, but that was under my grandmother's pressure, and you clearly know how bad that decision was. It was a mistake—one that clouded my judgement and went against my career."

I held his gaze unflinchingly.

"Your father warned us for a good reason. Relationships make us weak, Krish. They undermine our ability to make objective decisions for the sake of the mission and the greater good."

Krish started to protest, but I spoke over him. "I learned the hard way how selfish love can become. How it twists your priorities and makes you lose sight of your duty."

Shaking my head, I concluded, "I won't ignore those lessons and make the same errors again. You need to understand that I don't crave or require that kind of bond right now. My dedication is to my work and work alone."

My heart splintered, but I held firm.

"I can't, Krish. I'm sorry." The words felt like tearing off a limb.

Krish dropped my hand, looking utterly defeated, but the frustration on his face said that he wouldn't give up on this conversation yet.

"I've missed you every day you've been away," Krish replied. "I don't know if this is love yet. What I do know is that I care for you deeply. Being with you makes me happy in a way I've never felt before. These past months apart have been agonising. I missed your smile, your laugh, and your companionship every single day. I understand your reservations, but I can't simply ignore what's between us only because my primary focus now should be on my role in GLEN. If relationships hindered GLEN's success, only single and divorced individuals would be working for the organisation. GLEN is successful because we all know where to draw the boundaries between our personal and professional lives. A prime example is my father, the President of GLEN. He was married when he started GLEN, and his relationship with my mother never affected his commitment or responsibilities towards law enforcement."

The door swung open and Dr. Bhat entered, followed by my team leader, Sudesh, interrupting our charged moment.

I saw Krish straighten from the corner of my eye, stepping back from my bedside. His façade of professionalism slid back into place flawlessly.

"How are you feeling, Agent Choudhary?" Sudesh inquired.

"Much better. Thank you for rescuing me on time," I replied evenly.

Dr. Bhat examined my bandages and vitals. Seeing Dr. Bhat, I realised that I was in a hospital located within one of GLEN's facilities in Singapore. My team got me to Singapore from Malaysia, safely out of Max's reach. Otherwise, they would have got me treated in Malaysia as nearly every country in alliance with our organisation, dedicated to combating severe crimes, had infrastructures such as training centres, hospitals, safe houses, and more, specifically designed for agents like us. Dr. Bhat played a crucial role in GLEN's medical team, overseeing the physical and psychological preparedness of agents for their missions, but he only practiced at the Singapore headquarters.

"You've been very lucky, Trisha," he said. "The wound should heal in a few weeks."

Krish cleared his throat. "Doctor, could you give us a moment? I need to discuss the mission with Agent Trisha and Sudesh."

Dr. Bhat nodded and exited. As soon as he left, Krish rounded on Sudesh. "I want a full report detailing exactly how this mission went wrong on my desk in 48 hours."

Sudesh paled slightly. "Yes, Sir, of course." He turned to me almost pleadingly. "Trisha, can you walk me through your cover being compromised? Did Max or his men say anything indicating how they discovered your identity?"

I shook my head. "It all happened so fast... One minute everything seemed normal, and the next they were ready to kill me."

Sudesh sighed heavily. "Clearly, there was a leak of information somewhere. Don't worry, we'll get to the bottom of it."

"I'll assist you once I'm out of here," I said to Sudesh, but Krish shut me down coldly.

"You are barred from field work for two weeks, effective immediately, until medically cleared."

I bristled at Krish overruling me but held my tongue.

Sudesh awkwardly tried to smooth things over. "The, uh, standard recovery protocols make sense here. Your identity being compromised makes you the target of not just Max but his brother — the drug cartel kingpin we are after. Until we have a next plan of action, why don't you take this time to lay low?"

Ignoring him, Krish continued. "She'll stay at the GLEN safe house here in Singapore. Make the necessary arrangements, Sudesh."

"Sir, the safe house is already occupied by you and —"

"And Agent Trisha will share it with me until she's fit to rejoin."

Sudesh agreed easily, oblivious to Krish's underlying motives. I realised what Krish was doing — manoeuvering to get me alone and off duty, cleverly abusing his power to force us to confront this tension between us.

"You can't bench me like that. The mission failure was my responsibility as well. I must collaborate with my team to get to the roots of this."

Krish crossed his arms, his eyes glinted dangerously.

"These are my directives, Agent Trisha. No one challenges a Director's orders unless they wish to be permanently removed from this mission. I could easily assign someone else in your stead, not due to incompetence, but because you failed to adhere to the standard protocols of maintaining a low profile when compromised. Do you want that?"

Sensing the tension, Sudesh cleared his throat. "I'll, uh, go start safehouse preparations then." He couldn't wait to get out fast enough.

The moment we were alone, I faced off with Krish. "You can't threaten me like that, Krish."

Krish was unmoved. "I decide when my agents are fit for duty. And trust me, you'll thank me for this."

I wanted to rage at his patronising power play but knew it was futile. For now, Krish held all the cards.

"I believe you've had enough changes for one day to adapt to. I'm sending your meal after consulting with Dr. Bhat. Finish it before I return for Round 2 of our chit-chat."

My jaw dropped at his request. He had reverted to the Krish who enjoyed teasing and testing me. I fumed internally, then realised my hospital gown had slipped down, leaving me exposed. Clutching the fabric to my chest, I struggled awkwardly with my injured shoulder. I should have called the nurse, but before I could, Krish reached me to help.

"Here, let me." Ignoring my protests, he gently held the strings and stepped closer to tie them properly.

His knuckles grazing my bare skin sent shivers through me. I froze, heart pounding wildly as he secured the gown, his face inches from mine.

The intimacy of the gesture and the nearness of his body overwhelmed me. I knew my feelings were laid bare in that moment, my flustered state impossible to hide. Krish's knowing look as he pulled away confirmed it. I had revealed too much. Shown vulnerability I hadn't even fully admitted to myself. Now he saw the effect he had on me. My carefully built walls were crumbling, defences weakened by fatigue and emotion.

I broke eye contact, trying to steady my breathing as Krish walked out. How could I stay firm when he could unravel me so easily? This was dangerous—being alone together, barriers lowered. Feelings I had forcefully buried were bubbling back up. Feelings that could cloud my judgment again if I let them. I had to be stronger. Remind myself of the heartbreak that came with loving someone in this life. I would not lose myself that way again. But Krish had seen the cracks in my armour. Sensed the power he still held over me. And soon, we would be completely isolated.

Apprehension gripped me at what more might happen between us then. Could I trust myself to resist? Or would I fall back into his orbit, despite the cost?

KRISH

The moment I got the call that Trisha had been shot, my blood ran cold. Knowing Trisha was injured halfway across the world... tore me apart inside. Trisha had made it abundantly clear she didn't want me interfering in her life anymore—that shutting me out was necessary for her to succeed in her job role.

So, I respected her wishes, no matter how much it hurt. But when the call came about her being attacked and wounded, all my resolve shattered. Within an hour, I was on a plane to Singapore, protocols and promises be damned. The excuse I gave everyone about my presence in Singapore was about the mission fallout—assessing the damage and determining what went wrong—that my personal attachment to the injured agent didn't factor in.

But that was a lie. Seeing Trisha so pale and lifeless in that hospital bed wrecked me. I couldn't stay away simply to spare her pride or maintain distance. I needed to see her, needed to know she would be alright. And when Dr. Bhat told me Trisha was taking my name over and over again in her subconscious state, a flicker of hope sparked in me. Perhaps there was still a chance for us.

Taking her to the safehouse felt justified. It was for her own safety while recovering, or so I claimed. But truly, I engineered this situation to steal time alone with Trisha. Away from prying eyes, where we didn't have to be so guarded. Trisha could hate me for the manipulation, but saving our connection was more important now. Maybe we still had a chance, despite the odds. After all, my instincts had led me to her side when she needed me most.

Two days later, I pulled the car into the underground parking of the safehouse. It was in a quiet suburb on the outskirts of Singapore's bustling metropolis. Trisha gazed up curiously at the nondescript concrete building. To an outsider, it looked like any other apartment block, but I knew its anonymous exterior hid state-of-the-art security features inside.

We took the elevator up to the third floor, and I keyed in the code to unlock the door. Ushering Trisha inside, I watched her take in our home for the next two weeks until I deemed her fit for the mission again and until we found out what compromised the mission in the first place.

It was a modest two-bedroom flat, intentionally furnished in muted tones and devoid of any personal effects. But the space had everything we needed — a fully equipped kitchen, living area, and two separate bedrooms for us to maintain a level of privacy and distance.

Of course, I had arranged for all the medical equipment that would be needed to treat Trisha's injury and for her recovery before her arrival. But I also wanted her time here to be about more than that — reconnecting and lowering her defences around me.

While the nondescript safe house lacked warmth or character, but with Trisha by my side, I was determined to infuse it with warmth and possibility. Fill the sterile shell with laughter, memories, and understanding. Find our way back to the ease we'd shared before duty and protocol drove us apart. Maybe it was optimistic to think we could recapture what had slipped away. But I had to try. Being here, just the two of us removed from the scrutiny of GLEN, was the chance I had been waiting for. A glimpse of the bond we could nurture, if Trisha was willing.

CHAPTER 7 (LIGHT IN THE DARK)

MAX

The tumbler shattered against the wall, the amber liquid trickling down the expensive wallpaper. But I barely registered the mess, rage boiling inside me as Marco's words echoed in my mind. Trisha was alive. That two-faced snake, the woman I had trusted and cared for — she had played me this entire time.

"How can she still be alive?" I bellowed, grabbing Marco by the shirt. "You told me our men would find and finish her."

He shook his head desperately. "We tried, boss! Her team was too quick to hide her away. But our insider just confirmed she's holed up in some kind of safe house now, but not in Malaysia."

I shoved him backwards in disgust and began pacing like a caged tiger.

"Then where is she now?"

"Singapore," he replied.

Trisha, my beautiful Trisha, had been selling me out for god knows how long, feeding intel to the cops about our operations. Why else would our two big drug shipments have been intercepted recently? It had to be her. And I was too blind, too enamoured by those big doe eyes and playful smiles to realise I was being played — that she was an undercover agent implanted in my gang. But no more. Now, I saw her for the conniving viper she was. I would find where she was hiding and kill her myself. Watch the life drain from her eyes as I choked the breath from her lying throat.

She would pay for making me look like a fool, for betraying my trust and affection. I had opened up to her like no other, letting her see sides of myself no one else was privy to. And she had twisted it all to use it against me. My hands shook with the urge to wrap my hands around that delicate neck and squeeze until it snapped. I would find her, no matter where she cowered. And I would be the last person she ever saw once I dug my fingers into those big betraying eyes. She would regret the day she decided to make an enemy of me.

Because this wasn't just about wounded pride. If my brother Ron found out about this—about me being duped by an undercover agent—he would have my head on a platter. The great kingpin, brought down by his idiot younger brother's weakness for a pretty face.

No, I had to locate Trisha and eliminate her in a week before Ron arrived in Malaysia. He knew I liked Trisha and had been waiting to meet her from long. I could invent some story, pretend she had simply disappeared—as long as there was no living proof of how stupidly I had been played.

Turning back to Marco and the others, I straightened to my full height. "Find her location now. I don't care what it takes—hack security cameras, torture her contacts, pay off informants. Just bring her to me before my brother gets here."

They scrambled to obey as I poured myself another drink with shaky hands. I would give Trisha one last chance to impress me—with how gracefully she could beg for her life on her knees before I ended it. Then I would get rid of her for good. Because the time for games was over. She would regret stepping into my playground, thinking she could outwit me. I was the predator here. And she was nothing but my prey.

KRISH

It was our first morning together in the safe house. The previous night had passed uneventfully with us retreating to our respective rooms after polite but strained conversation. Then I took care of some phone calls with my team back in Austria, getting updates on other missions I'd my eyes on.

This morning felt different, more intimate somehow, our guards down in the soft morning light. I was scrambling eggs in the kitchen when I heard Trisha's door open. I glanced up and instantly froze. I couldn't tear my eyes away as I watched Trisha emerge fresh from the shower, hair damp, clad in just an oversized t-shirt that barely reached mid-thigh. She had worn it with denim shorts, flaunting her long, creamy legs. She stood there fresh from the shower, rivulets of water still glistening on her bare skin. Her hair was wrapped in a towel, a few damp tendrils framing her beautiful face. For a moment, I felt my heartbeat race on seeing her in this relaxed outfit. After months of seeing Trisha only in conservative work attire, her casual appearance now left me momentarily stunned. And undeniably aroused.

Those endless legs... the curve of her hips as she walked... the fluttering glimpse of collarbone peeking from the wide neck of the tee...

My heart pounded louder than a Dolby music system. Abruptly, I wrenched my gaze back to the eggs I was mauling as she caught me staring. Just act normal, I scolded myself. But I could still feel her presence like a lightning rod as she entered the kitchen.

"Who packed my bags for here?" she asked, sounding annoyed.

"Not me. Why?" I replied, puzzled.

"What do you mean why, Krish? There's barely anything decent in here," she huffed. "Just shorts and tees, like I'm on vacation."

I couldn't help chuckling. Trisha shot me a look.

"This is serious, Krish. I need some real outfits." she snapped.

"Sorry, but you should be thankful your team grabbed anything before getting you out of there. And you don't look half bad in these."

"I look like a clown." She rolled her eyes.

"Oh, come on, you look fine," I said lightly, then added before thinking, "Honestly, you look pretty sexy."

Trisha's eyes widened in surprise, so I quickly added, not wanting to offend her, "I... I mean, a sexy clown."

She again rolled her eyes and sighed.

"C'mon, Trisha. It's hardly a matter of two weeks."

"That's what I'm saying. Two whole weeks stuck in this stuff around you. Great," she muttered, regretting it immediately while I grinned.

She didn't mind wearing these revealing outfits that exposed more skin. Her concern wasn't about the clothes, but rather about my presence while she wore them.

"I mean..." she paused, swallowing the unease, and diverted the topic instead. "I'm hungry."

Smart woman!

"Have a seat, breakfast is almost ready." I gestured to the small kitchen table.

"No thanks, I can cook for myself," she waved me off.

I knew staying under one roof idea for the next few days was difficult for her, but I never thought she would turn down my offer to cook for us. Shrugging and letting her take over the breakfast duty, I moved aside. The pan was hot. Trisha tapped the egg against the marble surface with her left hand, ready to crack it into the pan for an omelette. However, as she prepared to do so, the pain shooting through her shoulder reminded her that her right hand was still out of commission due to the injury. She winced as she stretched her arm, feeling the discomfort and nervously looked at me.

"That bullet clearly affected your common sense too — you're in no shape to be cooking," I teased back.

Her eyes flashed at the teasing jab. "I'm perfectly capable. I just need..."

But she lingered off for a few seconds as I effortlessly cracked the eggs and began whisking before she continued the argument.

"You and I both know I'm still capable of handling missions, even in my current state. If your logical reasoning had been sharper, you wouldn't have sidelined me from fieldwork for two weeks. I miss being out there, Krish."

"Seriously?" I frowned. "When was the last time you took a break or went on a holiday?"

She didn't reply and sat on the chair at the counter. I slid the cooked omelette onto a plate, handing it to her.

"Careful, it's hot," I warned.

Our fingers brushed and lingered. The domesticity of this moment felt dangerously intimate. With supreme effort, I focused on plating the eggs and toast, trying not to notice the soft sound of Trisha's legs brushing together under the table, or the towel slipping slightly from her hair, revealing the smooth skin of her neck... Clearing my throat, I continued our previous debate.

"I've seen your records. You hardly take a break or get off work. Why is that?" I probed, eating from my plate.

"I like to keep myself busy."

"That means you don't like solitude?"

"Do you?" she countered.

"Nah! Nobody does. Want to know my trick for coping with loneliness?" I queried.

Trisha looked at me sceptically, but there was a hint of curiosity in her face. "Alright, what's your big secret trick for coping with solitude?"

I leaned in conspiratorially, thrilled by her closeness.

"It's pretty embarrassing, but..." I lowered my voice to a dramatic whisper. "I talk to myself."

Trisha's eyebrows shot up in surprise. Then, a smile tugged at her lips. "You talk to yourself?"

"Full-on conversations!" I said. "I'll take both sides of a debate or just narrate what I'm doing. The mailman probably thinks I'm crazy."

That elicited a laugh from Trisha, her eyes lighting up. "Do you use different voices and everything?"

"Oh, absolutely," I nodded earnestly. "I have a whole range of accents and characters. You should hear my Russian accent; it's a hoot."

Trisha was really laughing now, shaking her head at my antics. "You're ridiculous." But her tone was full of amusement.

I grinned, buoyed by her reaction. "Hey, it works! Give it a shot the next time you're lonely, and you'll see."

Our eyes held, and our smiles lingered. Just for a moment, the tension between us evaporated. There was only this shared laughter, this joy of being together. Maybe we couldn't define or act on this undefinable connection yet. But I would treasure these small, perfect moments of bonding, and the sound of Trisha's unrestrained laughter. For now, that was more than enough.

TRISHA

Next Day

I emerged from my room, restless and bored from too much resting. Wandering into the living area, I found Krish intently watching something on the large TV screen. As I moved closer, I realised it was footage from the night at the club when everything went wrong—when Max discovered I wasn't who I claimed to be.

"What are you doing?" I asked Krish.

He glanced over, pausing the video. "Reviewing the footage to see if I can spot anything about how your cover was blown," he explained, his jaw tight with determination.

Of course. Krish had taken it upon himself to uncover the mole who exposed me. He felt responsible, somehow.

"It had to be someone from within," I mused. "No outsider knew I was undercover."

Krish nodded. "My thoughts exactly. Let's watch what happens right before Max is informed."

He rewound the video to the moment when one of Max's men, Marco, stepped away to take a phone call. We watched closely as Marco moved to a secluded corner of the club and spoke with a figure in a dark hoodie.

"Who is he?" I asked urgently.

"Let's zoom in and find out." Krish enlarged the footage, adjusting the contrast. As the figure turned slightly, recognition jolted through me.

"That's Daniel!" I exclaimed. "He was our insider, giving us intel on the drug cartel." Shock coursed through me at the betrayal.

Krish's expression was grim. "Looks like he was playing both sides. Tipped off Max to save his own skin."

My mind reeled, trying to make sense of it. Daniel had seemed totally loyal to our cause. But he had sold me out in the end. The ultimate betrayal. Sensing my turmoil, Krish touched my shoulder gently.

"We'll find Daniel and make him pay for this. He won't get away with it."

His reassurance calmed me slightly. We now had a target for retribution. A loose end to tie up so we could find closure. I was more than eager to tackle the man responsible for nearly costing me my life and undermining months of careful undercover work.

I paced the room impatiently as Krish called Sudesh, my team leader, to assemble a team to bring Daniel in. That traitor had to pay for betraying us, for nearly getting me killed.

As soon as Krish hung up, I jumped in.

"I need to be part of the team that takes Daniel down."

Krish's eyes flashed angrily. "Absolutely not. You're benched, remember?"

"But I know Daniel better than anyone—his connections, his hideouts. I can help track him faster." I stood firm.

"You'll advise remotely, that's it," Krish said sharply.

Frustration boiled up in me. "You can't keep me sidelined! You can't stop me from being involved in bringing Daniel in, Krish," I insisted, feeling stubbornness rising. "This is *my* mission."

Krish moved closer, his voice softening. "Trisha, I know it's your mission…"

I cut him off as anger spilled over. "I need to fix this, Krish. The sooner we wind up this thing, the sooner I'll come out of that guilt. I can't just sit here uselessly after everything I sacrificed was destroyed."

Suddenly, Krish's hands were cupping my face, forcing me to look at him. "None of this is your fault," he implored. "You dedicated months undercover, and made incredible sacrifices. It was Daniel's betrayal that ruined things, not you."

I shook my head, a lump forming in my throat. "If I had just been more careful, suspected there was a mole…" My voice cracked as emotions spilled over.

Krish stepped closer. His touch was comforting and electrifying all at once.

"Don't do this to yourself," he murmured. "What's done is done. Now we pick up the pieces and keep fighting." He gently caressed my cheeks with his thumbs. "Together."

I blinked back tears, the warmth of his hands soothing away some of the sting. "I just need to fix this, Krish," I whispered. "Make it right again."

He nodded slowly. "I get it. And we will, I promise you. But you need to heal first." His eyes were full of compassion. "Guilt helps nothing and no one. All it does is eat away at you from the inside."

I let out a shaky breath, my frustration dissipating. Krish was right—self-blame wouldn't change what happened. All I could do was learn from it. With Krish by my side, I could handle anything.

When I looked back at him, his eyes dropped to my lips for a split second. His face was just inches away. *What were we doing?* Krish's hands cupped my face, forcing me to meet his intense gaze. My skin burned everywhere he touched me. We were standing so close I could feel the heat radiating from his body. My heart stuttered as I recognised the desire darkening his eyes.

If I moved even slightly, our lips would meet. The very air felt electrified with possibility. We were both breathing heavily, hearts racing like mad. This was dangerous, a point of no return. But I was helpless to pull away from the raw need reflected in his eyes. I involuntarily swayed closer, my lips parting reflexively as we hovered a hairsbreadth away.

I could see the battle playing out in Krish's eyes—longing wrestling with restraint. But as his gaze dropped to my mouth again, all I saw was raw desire. We were so close to that point of no return. Every cell in my body screamed to close those last few millimetres between us.

But just before our mouths met, panic pierced through the haze. I twisted out of Krish's grasp, my heart pounding in my chest. His hands dropped from my face. The spell broke as abruptly as it had formed. Without looking back, I raced to my room, slamming the door shut.

What were we about to do? I pressed my palms against my flushed cheeks. We very nearly crossed a line that could ruin everything. I paced my room, working to slow my ragged breathing. This staying under the same roof had brought out intense feelings in both of us. But I had to stay vigilant and remember what was at stake, despite the magnetic pull between us or how tempting it was to lose myself in Krish's arms.

CHAPTER 8 (SHOOT OUT)

KRISH

As Trisha ran away, the loss of her presence hit me like a physical blow. My hands dropped uselessly to my sides, still burning from the feel of her soft skin beneath them. For a dizzying moment, we had teetered on the edge, so close I could almost taste her lips. It took every ounce of restraint not to pull her back and press my mouth to hers. But then she was gone, the charged air between us turning cold in her absence. The slammed door echoed with sharp finality, leaving me alone with my ragged breathing and pounding heart.

Part of me, the part that had been longing for this moment for far too long, wanted to chase after her, to pull her into my arms and seal what we both knew was brewing between us with a kiss. It felt like the natural progression of things, the culmination of the undeniable chemistry that crackled between us whenever we were together.

But another part of me, the rational part, knew that Trisha wasn't ready for that. She was still grappling with the fallout of Daniel's betrayal, still burdened by guilt and self-blame. Pushing her into something she wasn't ready for would only complicate matters further, and I couldn't bear the thought of adding to her already heavy load.

I raked my hands through my hair in frustration as I stood there alone in the living area. The memory of her soft lips, tantalisingly close, lingered in the air. I couldn't shake the feeling that I had missed an opportunity, that I had let fear and uncertainty dictate my actions instead of following my heart.

But maybe it was for the best. Maybe this was a sign that we needed to take things slow, to let whatever was between us simmer and grow organically. And maybe, just maybe, when the time was right, Trisha would be ready to take that leap with me. Until then, I would wait patiently, knowing that our connection was too strong to ignore and too powerful to be denied.

****

The next two days buzzed with activity inside the safe house, even though it was just Trisha and me. We were constantly plotting and planning our mission to capture Daniel. The stakes were high, and time was of the essence. We knew we had to act before Daniel could get suspicious that we were coming for him.

The third day passed in a blur of video calls and strategy sessions. Our team, though remotely connected, was as involved as if they were right there in the safe house. The walls echoed with our voices, discussing, debating, and deciding the best course of action. We could track Daniel's location, just like we could track every movement of every agent in GLEN. His location still showed he was in Kuala Lumpur, which is why the team there was planning their mission to catch him. Daniel was a traitor, and we had to bring him to justice. Trisha and I poured over maps and surveillance footage, analysing every possible angle and every potential risk, determined to outsmart our adversary at every turn.

But amidst the chaos of this mission, there was another, more personal battle raging within me—the memory of our near-kiss haunting my every thought. I couldn't shake the image of Trisha's lips, so close yet so out of reach, the taste of what could have been lingering on the edges of my consciousness.

On the fourth day, I found myself watching Trisha as she sat cross-legged on a yoga mat, her eyes closed in meditation. She exuded an aura of calm and serenity, a stark contrast to the chaos that surrounded us. Lost in the moment, I failed to notice the pillar in my path until it was too late. With a loud thud, I collided with it, my balance lost as I stumbled backwards, landing unceremoniously on the floor.

Trisha's eyes flew open, concern etched on her features as she rushed to my side.

"Krish? Are you okay?" she asked, her voice laced with worry as she inspected the forming bruise on my forehead.

"I'm fine," I said, wincing as she gently touched the tender spot. "Just attacked by a rogue pillar."

Trisha chuckled, the sound felt like music to my ears. "You should have watched where you're going instead of blaming the pillar."

"Hey, I was walking in a perfectly straight line!" I protested. "It's not my fault the architect put that pillar right where people walk. Who does that? Hazardous design if you ask me."

Trisha rolled her eyes playfully. "Admit it, you just weren't paying attention. Your focus was elsewhere."

Now, I am stunned.

"Can you see with your eyes closed?" I asked, hoping she hadn't seen me openly admiring her doing meditation, the only reason why I couldn't see the pillar in my way.

"Nope," she replied, a smile playing on her lips. "But you are becoming pretty predictable these days, Director. It's not hard to guess why you couldn't see the pillar."

She knew I was ogling her during her meditation.

"Just another day in the life of Krish," I joked, flashing her a lopsided grin.

She rolled her eyes playfully, a smile tugging at the corners of her lips.

"You're lucky you didn't knock yourself out," she teased, blowing gently on my forehead bruise, a sign that she cared.

Our gazes locked, and for a moment, everything else faded away. It was a soft, intimate gesture, a respite from the harsh reality of our mission.

But the moment passed as quickly as it had come, reality crashing back in with a jolt. We had a job to do, a traitor to apprehend. Now wasn't the time to get distracted, no matter how we might feel.

With a sigh, Trisha stepped back, the professional mask slipping over her features once more. "Come on, let's get some ice on that." And just like that, we slipped back into mission mode, the job at hand taking priority. But that shared moment lingered, a spark kindling between us, waiting to ignite.

It was day seven. We'd been at it for hours, reviewing every scrap of intel on Max and his elder brother Ron's operation, searching in vain for some thread we could pull that might unravel the whole enterprise. My eyes were tired from staring at page after page until the words blurred together. The other team in Kuala Lumpur was ready to carry out the mission to arrest Daniel tomorrow.

Across from me on the couch, Trisha rubbed her neck, rolling her head side to side to try and relieve the tension.

"Ugh, I need a break," she muttered, "my brain is fried."

I knew the feeling. My own neck and shoulders were knotted tight as a drum. But I found myself distracted from my discomfort, watching a stray lock of dark hair curl softly against Trisha's cheek.

All I could think about was reaching across to tuck it back behind her ear, using it as an excuse to touch her skin.

Our eyes met and her lips parted slightly, a question in her expression. Ever since our missed kiss, the air between us felt charged, ready to ignite.

I looked down hurriedly, shuffling the messy pile of papers in front of me. "Yeah, let's take 15 to reset." I tried to sound casual.

We escaped to opposite sides of the apartment, apparently to clear our heads and stretch our cramped muscles. But before long, I found my eyes drifting down the hall to where Trisha stood gazing out the window, backlit by the setting sun. The light played over her delicate features, and I ached to go to her, to pick up where we'd left off. Focus, man, I told myself, shaking my head. But it was getting harder by the day.

Later, as we passed each other in the narrow hallway, her arm brushed against mine, sparking that electric current once more. We froze, our hungry eyes locked. For a dizzying moment, I thought she might lean in, might bring her lips to mine again. I swayed toward her, everything in me screaming to close the gap between us.

But once again, at the last second, Trisha blinked and turned away, a pretty blush blooming on her cheeks. With a ragged breath, she escaped to the living room. I braced my arm against the wall, knocking my head gently against it in frustration. *Get it together, Krish.* But my heart was racing as if I'd just defused a bomb.

This idea of staying under one roof had suddenly gotten a lot more dangerous. We were both fighting a losing battle here. The spark between us was bound to ignite into an alarm blaze. I wasn't sure if I had the strength or will to stop it. And looking into Trisha's eyes lately, I wasn't convinced she wanted me to.

****

Today was the day we had been waiting for — the day we would finally take down Daniel and get justice for all he had done. The team was in position, ready to move on his hideout in Kuala Lumpur on my command. Trisha and I were waiting anxiously for updates. But she also had a check-up scheduled with Dr. Bhatt to assess her shoulder injury from the earlier blowout. Despite her protests, I insisted on joining her at the hospital. Until Daniel, Max, and Ron were in custody, I refused to let her out of my sight. The guards accompanied us to the hospital, where I paced restlessly in the waiting room while the doctor examined her, keeping in touch with the ground team there in Kuala Lumpur headed by Sudesh.

Trisha emerged from the exam room, absently rubbing her shoulder. She looked at me expectantly.

"Any news?" she asked, eyes searching mine.

"The team is in position just a few blocks from Daniel's location," I updated her. "They're preparing to move in now. His tracker shows he hasn't left the compound."

Trisha nodded, looking relieved. "Hopefully, that means he has no idea what's coming."

"We are lucky," I agreed.

She flexed her shoulder gingerly. "I need to run to the market for a few things. Just some basic essentials."

"I'll join you," I said, readily walking her out, with the guards flanking us.

At the market, I stayed glued to Trisha's side, one eye constantly on the surroundings, one hand hovering near my weapon, just in case! My phone was constantly in a live call with Sudesh, the team leader in KL, so I could monitor the operation in real time.

"Sudesh, what's your status?" I asked tersely as we inspected vegetables at a stall. Trisha watched me closely, her face tensed.

"We've got the building surrounded and have started taking out exterior targets. Preparing to breach on your go-ahead."

"Proceed, but exercise extreme caution. I need Daniel alive." Trisha's eyes flickered with anticipation.

We purchased what we needed and moved on, the mundane task at odds with the knowledge that everything was coming to a head back in KL. My adrenaline was spiking, but I had to stay cool.

Another update came through from Sudesh. "Entry team is in. No hostiles on the first floor."

Trisha tensed and gripped my arm. I gave what I hoped was a reassuring nod. Suddenly, Sudesh screamed on the call.

"Ambush. Ambush. Get cover."

Gunfire echoed through the phone.

"Sudesh? What the f*ck is happening?" I screamed, my heart racing.

We hurried back towards the waiting car, the mission updates continuing in tandem.

Sudesh's voice came through, "Daniel is not here. There are a bunch of hostiles firing at us. They knew we were coming. They baited us with Daniel's tracker."

More firing sounded in the background, and the call got disconnected. If Daniel wasn't in Kuala Lumpur, where was he? Just when this thought crossed my mind, my guards screamed behind us.

"Sir, watch your six."

My soldier's instinct kicked in, and I gently pulled Trisha behind a stall, gesturing for her to stay low. Men with guns appeared, fanning out to block our exit. Trisha's eyes widened in alarm, but she kept silent, trusting my lead.

I cursed under my breath, angry at myself for letting our guard down and coming out in the open like this, putting us in harm's way. They were around ten men, and we were outnumbered and outgunned. Trisha was unarmed, while I only had my sidearm. It was clear—this was an ambush orchestrated by Max. His men must have been tracking us, waiting for an opportunity to strike.

Gunfire erupted, bullets ricocheting off the walls around us.

I shielded Trisha, firing back at the assailants. "Stay down!" I yelled over the deafening noise. We were sitting ducks if we stayed put. I had to get Trisha to safety.

During a lull in the shooting, I grabbed her hand and made a beeline towards a nearby building. More shots rang out. My guards covered us, firing back as we crashed behind the walls, letting it barricade us.

"That's Daniel and Marco," Trisha screamed, crouching down beside me. Marco was Max's right hand, his best man so far, his protector. And Daniel was with him, confirming he was a traitor who had made allies with the lawbreakers for God knows how long. But what were they doing in Singapore? They should have been in Malaysia. Did that mean Max was here too? F*ck!

"We can't stay here," I said, my voice tight with anxiety. The goons would be on us in minutes. I racked my brain for a way out. "Our car is on the other block. Let's try to get there, okay?"

Trisha nodded, holding my hand again. As soon as we tried running to the other block, the gunfire erupted once more. Marco yelled and pointed his men at us as soon as he saw us. I kept firing behind, taking down two of their men before we took cover behind a dumpster, using it as a shield again.

"Damn it!" Trisha cried out. I could see the fire in her eyes, the fighter in her, unwilling to be trapped like this. "Give me a gun, Krish!" she yelled.

I hesitated. Her wounded shoulder couldn't take the recoil. But I could see the determination on her face. She was a soldier to the core. With a grim nod, I called to my men positioned around the perimeter.

"Throw her a gun, now!" I commanded.

One of them flung a gun in our direction. Trisha caught it deftly and checked the clip. "Let's take these bastards down," she said.

I felt a swell of pride for this fierce, capable woman. We were in this fight together. We leapt out from cover, firing in tandem at our attackers. Marco's men scrambled for cover, surprised by our bold counterattack. Adrenaline pumped through my veins as we advanced through the alley, using parked cars and corners for cover, leapfrogging each other.

Finally, we had a clear line of sight of Marco and Daniel. Trisha steadied her aim on Daniel while I drew a bead on Marco. Her eyes were steely with determination. These were the men who had hurt her, had nearly killed her. Taking them down was personal. No words were needed between us. We fired simultaneously, our shots echoing through the alley as they found their marks. I watched as Daniel and Marco collapsed, the light leaving their eyes. My guards were taking down the remainder of Max's thugs at a distance. Trisha stood beside me, chest heaving with adrenaline and exertion, but thankfully unharmed. We had done it. We had survived the ambush and taken down two of Max's most trusted associates.

I turned to Trisha, needing to see for myself that she was alright after the harrowing firefight.

"Are you okay?" I asked urgently.

In response, she threw her arms around my neck, her body pressing tightly against mine. Before I could react, her lips came crashing down on mine, fierce and hungry. I couldn't determine whether it was the rush of adrenaline from narrowly escaping death or the satisfaction of successfully confronting the men who had thwarted her previous mission that prompted Trisha to kiss me. All I knew was that the taste of her mixed with gunpowder sent my senses reeling.

Instinct took over. I wrapped my arms tightly around her slender frame, crushing her body against mine as I returned her passion tenfold. Our tongues tangled together urgently, desperately, as months of pent-up tension finally exploded between us.

I slid one hand down her back, still clutching my gun, while my other hand threaded through her silky hair. I angled her head to deepen the kiss, claiming her mouth hungrily. She responded with equal fervour, moaning into my mouth as our bodies melded together. I could feel every curve pressed against me as she arched into my embrace.

Breaking the kiss to gasp for air, I trailed my lips down the graceful column of her neck. Her pulse hammered rapidly under my tongue. My hands roamed her back, tracing each contour as I pulled her impossibly closer, overcome with need.

Trisha clung to me just as fiercely, nails digging into my shoulders. Tilting her head, she guided my mouth to hers again in a dizzying kiss that seared through my entire being. Nothing existed in those moments but her body against mine, our pounding hearts beating in sync as we got lost in each other. This changed everything, but it felt so right.

CHAPTER 9 (ENEMY LINES)

TRISHA

My lips were still tingling from the urgent kiss we had just shared. I was the first to break away, gasping for air. Krish's dark eyes bored into mine, equally breathless. The tension that had been building between us for months had finally reached its breaking point.

I couldn't ignore it anymore—this magnetic pull I felt towards him. In the heat of battle, running on pure adrenaline, my body had acted on its own accord. But the truth was, I had wanted to kiss Krish for a long time. The urge had just been simmering under the surface until it finally boiled over.

Seeing him fight fiercely by my side to take down Daniel had stirred something primal in me. He was the only one I completely trusted to watch my back. Over time, he had become so much more than just my mentor or commanding officer. Krish was the person I relied on the most, someone I couldn't imagine being without.

As we stood there, time seemed to stand still while a thousand unspoken words passed between us. I knew I had crossed a line, but I didn't regret it. I was tired of resisting what I felt for this man. His strong, reassuring presence grounded me. His humour made me laugh when all seemed lost. His belief in me gave me strength.

I made my decision then and there to stop running from this connection between us. I didn't know where it would lead, but I was done pretending it didn't exist. My hand drifted up to caress his stubbled cheek gently as I gazed at him, heart thudding in my chest.

Just then, we heard the sounds of our team approaching. The charged moment was broken, and we reluctantly drew apart. It was time to get back to business. The battle was won for now, but the war still raged on.

Krish quickly resumed command, instructing the men to check the bodies and prepare to move out. I took a deep breath, steadying my nerves as I slipped back into mission mode. What had passed in those frenzied moments would have to wait.

As we made our way back to the safe house, Krish and I didn't speak of the kiss. But the memory of his lips on mine, his hard body pressed against me, lingered. I could still feel the ghost of his touch on my skin. Things had irrevocably changed between us. What it meant for our partnership going forward remained uncertain.

Yet, as we strategised over plans for our next move, I felt closer to Krish than ever. I trusted him completely, in every way. Together, we would keep fighting until Max and Ron were brought down.

****

The hot shower washed away the grime and exhaustion from the day's events. As the water cascaded over me, my mind replayed it all—the shootout, taking down Daniel and Marco, and that heated kiss with Krish. Just thinking about the feel of his lips on mine made my heart race all over again. I still couldn't believe I had been so brazen.

After towelling off, I slipped on my robe, my hair still dripping wet. The enticing aroma of stir-fried noodles wafted from the kitchen down the hall. My stomach rumbled, reminding me I hadn't eaten since early morning.

I followed the savoury scent to find Krish cooking up a late dinner, fully absorbed in his task. The domestic scene made me smile. His hair was also damp from the shower and he wore a soft grey tee that hugged his muscular frame. While keeping one eye on the wok, he spoke seriously into his phone. I caught the tail end of his conversation.

"Don't worry about that, Sudesh. I'll brief the directors on everything. Just send me the intel you have on Ron's movements so far. I'll need that."

Of course, he was already planning our next steps, coordinating with the team back in Kuala Lumpur. Krish never stopped strategising, determined to take down Max and Ron for good. It was part of what made him such a skilled agent and leader.

Before he could turn and notice me there, I crept up behind him, sliding my arms around his waist. He tensed in surprise before relaxing into my embrace. I splayed my fingers over his toned stomach, resting my cheek against his strong back. The clean, woodsy scent of his skin enveloped my senses.

Krish quickly wrapped up his call, covering my hand on his waist with his own briefly. When he turned to face me, his gaze travelled over my robe-clad form appreciatively.

"Dinner's ready," he murmured, brushing a wet lock of hair from my face. His fingers lingered, cupping my cheek with a tenderness that made me shiver.

We ate at the small kitchen table, knees occasionally bumping. A new energy hummed between us now. I caught Krish's heated looks over my glass of wine, no longer hiding his desire. After months of restraint, everything was bubbling to the surface.

I helped Krish clean up, our movements in easy sync. As we finished, he came up behind me at the sink, his hands circling my waist again as his lips found the sensitive spot below my ear. I leaned into him with a sigh, our bodies fitting seamlessly together. No more pretending we were just colleagues. The floodgates were open now.

We had crossed a line today, one that couldn't be erased. I turned in his embrace, meeting his mouth in a lingering kiss, silently promising more. Krish's kiss left me breathless, his hands burning trails of fire over my body. When we finally broke for air, he rested his forehead against mine.

"I was worried you'd retreat behind your walls again, pretend the kiss never happened," he admitted.

I caressed his stubbled jaw. "I'm done hiding how I feel, at least from you."

We both knew I'd still have to keep it under wraps from the outside world. But with Krish, I could finally stop holding back.

He captured my mouth again, kissing me deeply. My fingers threaded through his dark locks, pulling him closer. His hands roamed my back, tracing each contour as our tongues tangled. Every nerve ending was alive, my skin hyper sensitive everywhere he touched. His lips traced a heated path down my neck that had me gasping.

"Krish..." His name escaped as a moan.

He pulled back, his eyes dark with desire yet unsure. "What are we to each other now, Trisha?" His voice was rough.

I shook my head, tracing his sculpted lips with my fingers. "Let's not define this. I just know I want to be with you."

He looked puzzled by my reply.

"Naming it would mean expectations, boundaries that I am not yet ready to explore. What we share is special, Krish. But I also value the freedom and flexibility we have without the constraints of a defined relationship status."

I met his gaze, hoping he understood the depth of my feelings. "We have a long way to go, and I believe that journey will unfold naturally. We don't need to rush into labelling what we have. Right now, I'm content with the beautiful bubble we've created together, where we can simply be ourselves without any pressure or expectations."

"You think I wouldn't live up to your expectations?" he asked in a low voice.

"It's not you that I don't trust. It's me." I swallowed.

Krish searched my eyes, nodding slowly as understanding passed between us. Then he ducked his head, bringing his mouth back to mine.

Thanking God that Krish didn't press for the need to label our present relationship status, my hands roamed the hard planes of his chest as we kissed unhurriedly, our tongues dancing languidly. I could get lost in his taste, his touch. The outside world ceased to exist; there was only Krish and the exquisite sensations he awakened in me.

Without a delay, Krish lifted me off the floor and made me sit on the cool marble slab at the centre of the kitchen. My robe fell open, and his palms glided over my thighs, tugging the silk fabric up. I arched into him, craving more as he stood between my legs, hands skimming up my thighs, pushing the robe higher. My breath stuttered when his fingers stroked over my inner thighs. I rocked my hips, seeking more friction as delicious pressure built.

Tonight was just the beginning for us. We had crossed a line from work partners to lovers. But there were still so many firsts to share, and I wanted to cherish each one. I clung to him, trusting his lead. Krish's hands and lips on my body were pure bliss. The last thing I wanted was for this intimate moment between us to end. But the sharp shrill of my phone made me groan in frustration.

Krish reluctantly pulled back as I fished the offending device from my side. Sudesh's name flashed on the screen.

"You should take it. It could be important," Krish said, perceptive as always, even with desire still burning in his eyes.

I nodded, clearing my throat before answering. "Sudesh? What's up?"

"Hey Trisha, sorry to interrupt your time off. I know you're still recovering, but I could really use your help collating all the intel we have so far on Max and Ron's operations. Most of it is on your laptop from your earlier work."

I sighed, knowing this bubble had to burst eventually. "Sure, give me two minutes to get set up, and I'll meet you online to go over everything." With a promise to hurry, I ended the call.

Krish gave me a sympathetic smile, no doubt reading the disappointment on my face as duty called us back.

"We knew this was coming sooner or later," he said reasonably, brushing his fingers over my cheek. "But we have enough time; there's no rush for us."

His reassurance warmed me. He was right—we could pick this up again later. Maybe tomorrow. The mission still needed us. I nodded, leaning in for one more kiss before hopping down from the counter's edge. His hands steadied my waist, keeping me close a moment longer.

"Go be brilliant, like I know you are," he said with a grin.

I hurried to my room to retrieve the laptop and get set up at the table. My mind was still buzzing from Krish's touch, but I forced myself to focus. Sudesh needed my help making sense of all the disjointed intel on our targets' operations.

Soon, I was immersed in sifting through case files, cross-referencing sources, and connecting dots. The analytical part of my brain kicked into high gear. Krish checked on me briefly, dropping a kiss on my hair before returning to his room to attend to his own work.

It was nearly 3:00 a.m. when Sudesh and I finally signed off, a comprehensive report compiled for action. Exhaustion weighed heavily on me, but it was a productive session. And Krish was right— we had stolen these intimate moments together at last. There would be more.

I crawled into bed, thinking of his strong arms around me, his skillful hands awakening my senses. The memories kept my skin flushed and warm despite the late hour. This was just the beginning for us. And for now, I was content to let this bond between us grow at its own pace, undefined.

****

The harsh ringing of my phone jarred me awake. I fumbled for it, squinting against the bright morning light filtering through the curtains. Sudesh's name flashed on the screen again.

"Sudesh?" I mumbled, sitting up and raking a hand through my tangled hair. "What time is it?"

"Sorry, Trisha, I know it's early, but something urgent has come up," he said briskly. "You're being summoned to Phoenix HQ right away."

That got my attention. Our covert ops base—Phoenix Headquarters, in Singapore, was only contacted for the most serious matters.

"What's going on? Is it about yesterday?"

"Yes. Director Shergill is here—he flew in to take over the operation."

I sucked in a breath. Ayaan Shergill? I knew he was one of the Directors of GLEN and headed all of GLEN's field activity from Austria. If he was here, this had just got escalated to the highest levels.

"I'm on my way," I told Sudesh, urgency flooding my system now.

I quickly washed up and got dressed, my mind racing. Stepping out of my room, I found a note from Krish on his neatly made bed. He'd already left for Phoenix HQ himself. Of course, he would be a part of this briefing. He probably hadn't thought I would be called there, too, considering Krish had benched me for two weeks.

The guards escorted me out to the armoured SUV. At the nondescript building that served as our base, I was whisked through security and into the situation room. Sudesh and the others followed behind me. And just when I was looking for Krish, I saw him entering the room with Director Ayaan Shergill himself.

I recalled Krish mentioning his childhood friend Ayaan Shergill before. They had joined GLEN together, rising up the ranks due to their formidable skills and unshakable bond. While Krish excelled in operations, Ayaan's strength lay in his intuitions, and hence, he was involved in the criminal intelligence gathering and strategy.

Now, seeing Ayaan Shergill in person, I understood why he commanded such power and respect. He had a magnetic presence—

confident, dashing, with sharp eyes that missed nothing. I could see why Krish trusted him deeply. They made a great team.

As we took our seats, Krish's gaze found mine, his expression curious. He likely hadn't expected me to be summoned here too. His eyes softened for a split second before the man I assumed was Ayaan stood up to address us.

"For those I haven't met yet, I'm Ayaan Shergill, Director of Criminal Intelligence Operations at GLEN HQ in Austria." His voice rang with crisp authority. "You all have done outstanding work in dismantling this cartel bit by bit so far. I'm honoured to be joining the effort to deliver the final blow."

Murmurs of greeting went around the table at his introduction. He commanded the room effortlessly, his presence both formidable and reassuring.

"Now that we've taken out, Marco, Max's right hand, it's time to strike at the heart—Ron." Ayaan's voice was crisp with authority. "New intel confirms Max is holing up in Kuala Lumpur. My sources say Ron will be joining him tomorrow. That's our window to end this, once and for all..."

He went on to outline the plan, his sharp eyes missing nothing. With Ayaan Shergill on board, I knew we had a real chance at completing our mission. His confidence was infectious.

"You're forgetting one thing," Krish interrupted. "We still don't know where Ron and Max will be meeting. Only Max has that intel."

Ayaan smiled lightly. "You are right. That's why we need someone on the inside." His intense gaze turned to me. "You must be Agent Trisha, right?"

I stood up. "Yes, Sir."

"You've done outstanding work so far, Trisha. But we need you one more time."

I straightened, ready for anything he would ask of me.

"Just tell me what the plan is, Sir."

Ayaan turned to the rest of the team.

"Tailing Max covertly is likely impossible at this point. But we can track Trisha's movements if she intentionally crosses enemy lines and gets taken," Ayaan mentioned.

Before I could respond, Krish spoke up sharply. "What exactly do you need her to do? Get captured on purpose?"

"We're going to use her as bait to get to Max. Once he has her as a hostage, he'll certainly take her to Ron. That's how we track their location and take them both down."

It was risky but tactically brilliant. Before I could agree, Krish cut in sharply. "Absolutely not. It's too dangerous."

I bristled, about to protest that it wasn't his call, but Ayaan countered.

"It's the only sure way to get both targets in one strike. Trisha has proven herself more than capable. With our tracking chip implanted in her, she'd lead us right to them."

I saw the logic in the plan. "I'm ready to do what's needed, Sir."

But Krish cut me off again. "I won't allow Trisha to risk herself like that again." His protective stance surprised me. We were agents. This was our mission.

Ayaan held up a hand diplomatically. "Trisha, it's up to you whether to accept the mission or not." His tone made it clear what he hoped I'd choose.

"Ayaan, a word?" Krish interrupted.

I shot Krish a defiant look. The choice was mine, not his. But his eyes pleaded with me to refuse. Ayaan and Krish stepped aside, speaking in hushed tones. I watched Krish's profile, seeing the tension in his shoulders. He didn't like this one bit. But I would do it. We're so close to ending this. One final mission, and it would all be over.

CHAPTER 10 (TURNING POINT)

KRISH

As soon as Ayaan outlined his plan to use Trisha as bait, my heart clenched in dread. Sending her directly into Max's clutches again? After everything she'd already endured at their hands? It was unimaginable.

I gripped Ayaan's arm and pulled him aside, unable to contain my anger.

"Are you out of your mind? I won't allow Trisha to put herself in that kind of danger."

Ayaan regarded me steadily, unmoved by my outburst. We'd been friends for too long.

"I get your concern, Krish. But do we really have a better choice here? Ron won't surface unless he thinks he's meeting Max. And the only person who can get us close enough is Trisha."

I scrubbed a hand down my face, frustration bubbling up.

"You sound awfully casual about sending her off as fucking bait to those psychopaths. Have you forgotten what Max did to her before?"

Ayaan's expression softened a fraction. "Of course, I haven't. You think I'd ever put her life at risk unnecessarily?" He gripped my shoulder firmly. "I'm not here just as the Intelligence Director but also as your friend. If you don't want me to intervene in your decision to lead this mission, I won't. But after yesterday's ambush, I wanted to be sure you had all the support you needed to finish this. I can back off if you have a better plan than this."

I blew out a harsh breath, reining in my emotions at his words. Ayaan was right—I couldn't let my personal feelings cloud my judgment on this mission. He was only trying to help achieve our goal as effectively as possible.

"I know," I admitted gruffly. "And I'm grateful you're here. The truth is, I hate having to deploy Trisha as bait like this. It goes against every protective instinct I have."

"Trust me, we can do this," he replied.

I nodded in agreement.

"I hope it does. And honestly, action doesn't suit me like it does you," I added. "I've always been better in handling the technical side rather than being the man of action on the ground."

"Exactly," Ayaan grinned. "That's why we make such a good team. So, leave the cowboy heroics to me while you work your computer magic in the van."

I couldn't help but chuckle wryly at his friendly jibe. Since our early days at GLEN, Ayaan had always thrived in the field, while I preferred being tactical command. It was what made us such an efficient duo, balancing each other's strengths.

Clasping his shoulder, I met Ayaan's gaze seriously. "Just promise me you'll keep Trisha safe while she's in there."

It was only after I said those words that it clicked in my head that Ayaan would question my sudden affinity towards Trisha. So, before he could question me further, I explained.

"She is a friend now. And I don't want her hurt."

Ayaan's expression sobered. "You have my word, buddy. I'll protect her with my life if needed, just as I know you'd have mine."

With a nod of understanding passing between us, I felt the knot in my chest loosen. If anyone could watch over Trisha in a situation like this, it was Ayaan. He had never failed a mission or left someone behind. I trusted him implicitly.

"Alright, let's do this," I said, feeling calmer now. "Though, for the record, I still think this plan is moot. We're basically gift-wrapping Trisha and handing her over to that sadistic bastard Max."

Ayaan barked out a laugh, slapping me on the back. "There's the paranoid worrywart I know and love. That's why you're leading this op and I'm just here to provide support."

I rolled my eyes good-naturedly, relaxing into the easy camaraderie between us. "Yeah, yeah. Just don't go getting yourself blown up out there. Who else would I hang out with in Austria once we return otherwise?"

Ayaan chuckled heartily. "I practically saved your scrawny ass all the time, so a little respect is in order. Now come on, we've got work to do."

As we rejoined the others, I felt a sense of calm focus settle over me, the anxiety pushed aside. With Ayaan at my side and Trisha's combat abilities, we could pull this off and finally end Max and Ron's reign of terror once and for all.

****

The hours leading up to the operation were a flurry of activity. Ayaan was off and running, coordinating with local assets to gather the final intel on Max's compound and any potential locations where he might meet with Ron. My role was tactical planning and logistics — mapping out routes, positioning strike teams, and going over contingencies.

Trisha stayed close by for most of it, preparing herself. But we barely had a moment alone, always surrounded by the other agents and teams of the command centre we'd set up. Whenever our eyes met, I saw the same determined resolution reflected back at me, tinged with an undercurrent of anxiety.

Tomorrow, she would purposefully put herself in unimaginable danger once again. The thought made my chest tighten, but I ruthlessly pushed those feelings aside. She was also not thrilled that I'd tried to decide for her in front of Ayaan and the team by rejecting the idea of using her as bait to reach Ron. But what else did she expect? I wanted her safe. Was that so hard to understand?

That night, before we flew to Kuala Lumpur for the operation, Ayaan gathered everyone for the final briefing.

"Our intelligence has Max's location pinned down here," he said, pointing to a dilapidated area on the outskirts of KL on the map. "He's been lying low, likely waiting for Ron's arrival."

My stomach twisted at the thought of Trisha walking into that den alone. But this was the only way. I felt her gaze on me and forced myself to remain stoic as Ayaan continued.

"We have two objectives — finding Max and using him to lure out Ron. Once Trisha makes contact with the target, we'll have her location via the chip's signal. Then it's just a matter of moving in swiftly before they can bolt."

I studied the area maps intently, analysing potential routes and block points for the raid teams. Laying out the tactical plan helped me regain my focus. This was just another op, nothing more. I refused to let emotions cloud my judgment and potentially jeopardise Trisha's safety further.

Finally, it was time to deploy. Trisha was being outfitted with the tracking chip bio-monitors while Ayaan did the last weapons checks. Motioning her over, I pulled her aside for a rare moment of privacy.

"This is it," I said gruffly, struggling to keep my tone impersonal. "You know what you have to do?"

"Of course." Her eyes shone with determination, though a hint of vulnerability peeked through. "But if anything goes sideways in there..."

"It won't," I insisted, perhaps too harshly. I had to believe that. I couldn't let doubt creep in now. "Just get us a fix on Ron's location through Max. Ayaan and I will handle the rest."

I held Trisha's gaze, my throat constricting with everything left unspoken between us. This was it—potentially our final moment together before she walked into the lion's den once more.

"Trisha..." My voice cracked with the weight of all I couldn't say.

Before I could form any other words, she reached up and pulled my face down to hers in a searing kiss. Our lips met with an urgency born of desperation and longing. I froze for only a split second before melting against her, pouring every ounce of emotion I'd been holding back into the embrace.

My arms wound around her slender frame, holding her flush against me as our mouths moved in frantic synchrony. One of my hands slid up the curve of her spine to cup the back of her head, angling her to deepen the kiss further. Our tongues danced and duelled with rising intensity.

In that endless moment, the roar of the command centre here at Phoenix Headquarters faded away. There was only the scorching heat of Trisha's body against mine, the rapid faltering of our mingled breaths, and the velvet crush of her lips. I drank her in like a man dying of thirst, losing myself in the profound intimacy of our connection.

Finally, the need for air forced us apart, our foreheads pressed together as we panted harshly. Trisha's dark eyes were glazed with desire, her cheeks flushed. Sliding one hand up to cradle her face tenderly, I brushed my thumb over her feverish skin, tracing the curve of her cheekbones as if committing them to memory.

"Come back to me," I rasped, the words tasting of desperation and promise.

A ghost of a smile curved her lips as she leaned in to plant one last, achingly soft kiss over my mouth. "I will."

Then, she slipped from my arms and disappeared around the corner to rejoin the others before we could be discovered. I sagged back against the wall, chest heaving, body still thrumming with the aftershocks of that heated exchange. "Get it together, man," I chided myself sternly. Now wasn't the time for any other thoughts. Trisha's life was on the line, depending on me to have my head in the game.

Pushing aside the lingering taste of her lips, I headed for the command centre. My movements were steady, my mind clear and focused. It was time to lock away the man who loved her and revert back to the operative she could rely on without question. No matter what awaited her within Max's lair, I would stop at nothing to ensure Trisha emerged from it unscathed. Even if it cost me everything, I would bring her home.

TRISHA

<u>Next Day - Kuala Lumpur</u>

My heart pounded violently as I slipped through the dilapidated doorway of Max's compound. I was walking straight into the viper's den, alone and unarmed, except for the tracking chip embedded beneath my skin. One wrong move, and it could blow this whole operation sky high.

But we were out of options to find Ron. Using me as bait to draw out Max and then trail him to his brother was our last gambit. Krish had been vehemently against it at first until Ayaan talked him around. I knew Krish was terrified of me being captured again. But I was determined to see this through, no matter the risk.

Creeping down the dim hallway, my senses were on high alert for any sign of movement. Finally, I reached what appeared to be Max's makeshift office area. Taking a steadying breath, I stepped into the open doorway, pistol raised.

"Don't move," I barked as Max turned, startled, from where he stood at his desk. "Hands where I can see them."

His eyes widened in shock before narrowing menacingly. "Well, well. It seems the little spy has a death wish."

"The only one dying today is you," I spat. "After the stunt you pulled sending Daniel and Marco to kill me in Singapore, you're lucky I didn't put a bullet in you right here."

"Is that so?" Max's tone dripped with disdain. "If you had the guts to do it, you would've done it already instead of talking to me."

He was right—I had no intention of actually pulling the trigger. Not yet anyway. I had to stretch this out, make him think I'd come here to take revenge, and then get overpowered by his men on purpose, until Max took me right to Ron.

"You're not worth getting blood on my shoes," I sneered. "I've been ordered to arrest you alive. Although, I'll enjoy watching the light leave your eyes."

Right on cue, two of Max's henchmen burst into the room, drawn by the commotion. They rushed me from behind, grappling for the gun. The pistol went skittering across the floor as they wrestled me down, slamming my face into the dirty concrete. White-hot pain flared in my cheek as one of the bullies pressed my head against the ground with brutal force. I allowed myself to be overpowered, putting up just enough of a fight to seem convincing.

"Enough!" Max's sharp command made them back off slightly, allowing me to draw in a ragged breath.

With a nod from their boss, one of the men hauled me up by my hair, the strands ripping from my scalp. I cried out at the sudden agony. My legs threatened to give way, but the grip on my hair kept me upright.

"Well, now," Max's smug voice slid over me like oil. "Looks like the spy in you is too overconfident of her abilities, hmm?"

He stepped up, cool fingertips trailing over the burning wound rising on my cheek. I wanted to recoil, but he yanked my head back ruthlessly. Black spots swam in my vision from the shooting pain.

"Did you really think you could waltz in here and try to take me out?" Max chuckled darkly. "You're even more dumb than I thought. Luckily for you, I'm not gonna kill you just yet, Trisha."

His hand closed around my throat, and fear shot through me. I hadn't anticipated how swiftly things could escalate. I still needed to maintain his belief that I had failed and this was not just a ploy.

"Ron has been wanting to meet the spy bitch who made such a fool of me," Max hissed into my ear, his lips brushing against my lobe.

"He'll want to personally deal with you for getting Marco, our best man, killed before we return the favour."

Adrenaline spiked through my veins at the thought of being taken to Ron's lair. This was it — the moment we'd been working towards all along. Now, I just had to survive whatever torment was coming first.

Laughing viciously, Max gripped my hair tighter, forcing my head back painfully. My scalp felt like it was being ripped from my skull.

"But before we hand you over, I get to make up for all those months you played me. You didn't let me touch you back then… but now… how will you save yourself, Trisha?"

Revulsion churned in my gut at his meaning, his hot breath on my face. I expected him to strike, violate, and hurt me in every way imaginable. Maintaining my cover was one thing, but this…?

A call on Max's mobile diverted his attention momentarily from me. I took a sigh of relief as he answered, his gaze fixed on me.

"We have caught the spy," he said into the phone. "I'm bringing her to you soon."

He must be speaking to Ron, his brother. Even though the call wasn't on speaker mode, I could still hear Ron's voice. He commanded Max not to waste time and to bring me to him urgently. Ron was worried that if I was here, my other agents could track me down at any moment and secure this place. So, he specifically asked Max to start immediately.

However, it gave me some relief knowing that this might deter Max from carrying out his plans of touching me and violating me anymore. Not that I couldn't handle it. If I could safeguard myself all those months when I pretended to be his woman, I could do anything to protect myself even now.

Max reluctantly agreed with his brother and then disconnected the call, barking at his men to prepare for leaving.

A flicker of movement in my periphery made my blood run cold. Out of the corner of my eye, I glimpsed one of Max's thugs holding a scanning device, running it slowly over my body.

No… they couldn't be looking for…

"Let's find out if our little spy is wired?" Max's mocking voice dripped with cruel satisfaction.

My thundering heart felt like it would beat out of my chest. If they found the tracking chip, it was all over. No, I couldn't let them take this chance.

"You'll never find anything," I rasped out defiantly.

Max leaned in so close I could smell his foul breath. "Is that so? Don't worry; we will find out in no time."

One rough hand jerked up the sleeve of my shirt while the other gripped my forearm, immobilising me. The thug with the scanner passed it over my bare skin, his eyes focused on his task.

I held my breath, stifling the scream that threatened to escape as the device swept down to my upper arm... right over the embedded chip. Please, no. God, no...

There was a tense pause in the room, everyone frozen in anticipation. My muscles locked, bracing for the worst. Then, the rhythmic beeping of the scanner echoed like a death sentence. My tracking chip was traced!!

KRISH

The surveillance monitors flickered suddenly, static filling the screens. My heart plummeted into my stomach as an ominous silence filled the van, parked a few blocks away from Max's hideout where Trisha was supposed to be.

"We've lost her signal."

The words rang hollow in my ears. I fought to keep my composure, but dread and panic clawed at my insides.

"What the hell do you mean we've lost her?" I turned sharply to one of my men, who was tracking Trisha on the laptop, unable to mask the desperation in my voice.

"Where's Trisha's locator ping? We need to get a fix on her now!" Ayaan asked him, meeting my wild gaze with a resolute expression, his jaw set in a grim line. Furiously, I typed furiously on the array of computers before me. But no matter what I did, Trisha's tracking data remained stubbornly blank. My hands clenched into white-knuckled fists.

"They must have found the chip and disabled it somehow," Ayaan yelled.

My worst nightmare was unfolding right before my eyes — Trisha captured and defenceless in Max's clutches.

A string of curses erupted from my lips. We were blind, with no way of tracking her location or status. What were they doing to her? Just the thought of that sadistic bastard laying a hand on her made my vision bleed red.

"I have to go in after her," I growled, making for the exit hatch. But Ayaan's hand clamped down on my shoulder, halting me in my tracks.

"Not you," he said in a tone that brooked no argument. Gone was the easygoing friend, replaced by the hardened operative holding me back.

Furious, I nearly shoved him off, but the logical part of me took over as he explained further.

"We need someone on the ground to be our eyes and ears, Krish. I'll go in," he added.

Ayaan's gaze was steely, but I saw the glint of determination there—the same resolve that had pushed us through countless missions together.

"Keep those monitors locked on me." With that, he tapped the black beaded bracelet on his wrist—a plain decorative piece hiding his standard tracking device. Ayaan turned on his heel and exited the van.

All I could do now was breathe carefully and prepare for the storm that was about to break. I prayed with everything I had that we weren't too late to save the woman who meant everything to me.

CHAPTER 11 (SAME OLD SCARS)

TRISHA

The ropes dug into my wrists as I struggled against the restraints. Max's goons had tied me up tightly, leaving no room for escape. A grimy rag filled my mouth, muffling any cries for help. Worse, blood trickled down my right arm, where they had cut me open to remove the tracking chip embedded under my skin. Without that chip, how would my team at GLEN ever find me?

This solo mission to take down the notorious drug kingpin Ron and his brother Max was rapidly dooming. The plan had been to infiltrate their operation, gather Ron's hideout details, and coordinate an extraction, with full backup from headquarters. Instead, I'd been captured and stripped of my communication lifeline.

My heart pounded as Max's men hauled me outside and shoved me into the backseat of a waiting sedan. I landed with a grunt, twisting to avoid smashing my face against the door panel. One of the thugs slammed the door shut, bathing the interior in darkness.

The engine rumbled to life as Max climbed into the front passenger seat. He twisted around, a cruel smile stretching across his scarred face.

"Your death wish is gonna be fulfilled soon, woman."

A jolt of fear lanced through me. I jerked against the rope bindings in a futile attempt to loosen them. Max's raspy laugh echoed around me, mocking my efforts.

Taking me to Ron meant they intended to interrogate me first before the inevitable execution. My only hope was to withstand whatever torture they had planned long enough for my team to somehow track me down and launch a rescue. The prospect seemed impossible now that my locator chip was gone.

Our mission parameters were clear—we needed Ron alive to extract details about the higher tiers of this massive drug smuggling operation. As the cartel's kingpin, Ron held the key to the entire criminal hierarchy that had gone unchecked for decades. My secondary objective was simple: take out Max by any means necessary.

But the most daunting reality was surviving long enough to even attempt either of those goals now that I was at their mercy. Without backup, the odds of walking out of Ron's den were negligible at best, even if I miraculously managed to eliminate Max's men and their boss. Max handed over the location details on his iPad to the driver, commanding him to take us there. *To Ron's hideout!* An icy knot clenched my gut as the car accelerated away.

I strained against my bonds again, refusing to surrender despite the overwhelming odds. My mind raced, calculating every potential scenario, and analysing escape routes that no longer existed without my team's support.

The trunk shifted as we rounded a corner, the distinctive clinking of weapons accompanying the motion. I could tell there was extra ammunition in the trunk from the clinking. My jaw tightened behind the gag, every ounce of my training fortifying my resolve. I would not go down without a fight, no matter how hopeless the situation seemed.

The car rolled to a stop, the abrupt halt jostling me against the door panel. I tensed, expecting Max's thugs to haul me out and into Ron's stronghold — my odds of survival dipping with every passing second.

Instead, it was the driver who flung open the door, harsh sunlight invading the dim interior. I squinted against the glare as he reached in and grabbed my arm, yanking me from the backseat. Instinctively, I began thrashing, determined to resist even as the ropes bit into my wrists.

That's when I felt something small and hard being pressed into my bound hands.

I froze, fingers curling around the object as the driver leaned in close. His jaw was obscured by a mask, but the gruff whisper was unmistakable.

"Got your back..."

Ayaan Shergill?

Relief washed over me, followed swiftly by elation. Our comms might have been blocked, but the director of GLEN had somehow managed to infiltrate the operation to provide backup. He must have neutralised Max's original driver and taken his place to get this close without arousing suspicion.

As the other henchmen piled out, gloating over having captured me, Ayaan slipped back. They didn't pay him any heed. To them, he was just the hired driver, expected to hang back while they delivered their prize to Ron. My mouth twitched into a smile behind the gag. If they only knew the truth...

"Let's take her inside," Max growled, grabbing my arm in a vice-like grip.

The rest of his men followed suit. I allowed myself to be dragged away, knowing that Ayaan was watching over me from the shadows. There were no windows, just a single weathered door to this building—the perfect secret hideout for Ron. I made a show of struggling, keeping up appearances for our audience even as my fingers deftly worked the object Ayaan had slipped into my hands.

A pocket knife. He'd given me a weapon. I nearly sobbed with gratitude. And I trusted Ayaan to have a backup plan. The man worked entirely on instinct. By now, he'd have contingencies mapped out, and exit strategies ready. All I had to do was take out the immediate threat while he covered our withdrawal. Ayaan might have also informed Krish and our team of our present location. In minutes, they would be here to tackle the men and take them down one by one. The mere thought of some action kicked my adrenaline.

The plan started coming together in my mind even as Max shoved me toward the entrance, sneering all the while. Let the bastards think they'd won—it would make their defeat all the more embarrassing.

Once I had my eyes on our target, Ron, the kingpin of this drug cartel we'd been chasing all long, I would cut myself free and spring into action. I had one objective: eliminate Max's men and subdue Ron so Ayaan could back me up until our extraction team reached here and secured this area.

Max's grip tightened around my arm as he hauled me into the dimly lit main hall of the hideout. I stumbled along, playing the part of the captured prisoner even as my senses remained on high alert.

More of Ron's henchmen lined the walls, their grips tightening on their weapons as we entered. I made a silent tally—just fourteen, no, fifteen armed muscle heads providing security for their elusive kingpin? If it came to a fight, Ayaan and I would have our hands full, but nothing we couldn't handle.

Now if only the man himself would make an appearance...

As if on cue, a side door creaked open, and a hulk-like silhouette emerged from the shadows. Broad shoulders filled the frame; more solid muscle than I'd anticipated. It was Ron—the elusive target we had pursued through photos but had never met face-to-face.

He stepped fully into the main room, the overhead lights letting me see him clearly. An ugly scar cut across his cheek and jawline—a reminder of a life of violence, no doubt. He wore it like a badge of honour, his expression twisted into a sneer of disdain. This was a man who delighted in intimidating others through brute force.

My jaw clenched as Max released me, striding over to greet his brother with a jovial air.

"Brother!" The two men embraced with exaggerated back slaps.

Ron's cold stare remained locked on me over Max's shoulder, though.

"Look what I have for you," Max beamed, finally breaking away to gesture grandly in my direction.

The drug lord's face contorted with a mix of disgust and contempt.

"How can you be such a fool, Max? How could you be fooled by this woman all this time? It's written all over her face that she's a spy. How could you not notice?"

My heart skipped a beat at the acknowledgement. He was definitely smarter than Max. I prepared for the punishment that was surely coming, shifting my weight into a defensive stance.

Max hung his head, clearly displeased by the rebuke in front of his men.

"It's because of you we've lost Marco and a valuable insider like Daniel, who kept us informed on GLEN's progress."

Ron levelled an accusatory finger at me. Silence hung thick in the air as all eyes swivelled toward their boss as glared at me furiously. With two long strides, Ron closed the distance between us until I could smell the cheap whiskey souring his breath.

"I'll enjoy cutting you into pieces myself," Ron hissed through clenched teeth, "before packing them off to your headquarters as a lesson for the other agents to know what happens when someone messes with me."

Revulsion churned in my gut at his words, but I refused to show fear. I couldn't give him that satisfaction. Instead, I mustered my courage and met Ron's hateful glare with a taunting grin.

The reaction clearly wasn't what he'd expected. Surprise flashed across his features before the sneer resettled into place.

"I'm not joking, lady." He grabbed my chin in a vice-like grip, forcing my face even closer to his. "What the hell are you smiling for?"

"I'm smiling because I know what's about to happen in the next few seconds," I replied, unable to resist goading him further.

Ron blinked, momentarily thrown off balance. His confusion provided the critical opening I needed. With a swift motion, I planted my foot and wrenched out of his grasp, driving my knee up towards his gut.

He grunted in pain, instinctively hunching over to protect his midsection. I used the blade Ayaan had slipped me, slicing cleanly through the ropes around my wrists. Before Ron could recover, Max lunged at me. In one fluid motion, I whirled and slit his throat. Ron stared at me in horror as Max's body fell on the ground next to me.

"Max…" Ron's scream echoed in the room, a howl of anguish that drowned out the clatter of guns as his men scrambled to react.

I didn't wait for Max's crew to start firing at me. Dropping into a crouching position, I spun, kicked and sliced the throat of another one of Max's men. And that's when the sound of a gunshot firing from behind me echoed around. Ayaan was inside. He probably must have taken the guns and ammunition from the trunk of the same car we all came in from, the clinking sounds of those weapons I'd heard while driving to this place. Finding cover, I caught the flying gun which Ayaan threw in my direction to get into action.

Survival instincts honed through years of training took over, my body moving of its own accord. I ducked and weaved through the hail of gunfire, firing back. I fought back a grin as one of Ron's men crumpled, neutralised by Ayaan's precise shot.

No time to celebrate, not with the rest of the security rapidly regaining their focus. I seized another discarded pistol from the floor and opened fire, eliminating another two hostiles.

Diving into a sheltered nook, I risked a glance around the edge and spotted Ron crouched behind a structural pillar, his men forming a protective umbrella around their leader.

A distant whirring sound reached my ears—unmistakably that was the approaching helicopter. My heart plummeted into my stomach. Ron had called for air evacuation, and judging from the sound, it was already inbound.

The mission parameters scrolled through my mind. As a top priority, we needed Ron alive. That meant I had to take him into custody before that chopper touched down.

"Ayaan!" I shouted over the gunfire. "I'm going after Ron. Cover me."

An acknowledging nod was all he gave in between his firing. Grabbing a sidearm, I vaulted over the table and opened fire around the pillar at the men surrounding Ron. But my bullets were soon over than I thought. Throwing the gun, I rushed at Ron's men and knocked down one of them with a vicious kick before whirling to engage the other in hand-to-hand combat. Muscle fight was my thing, and I loved it more than using the weapons. But for now, I didn't want to let Ron get away. While I kicked and punched his men, Ron made a dash for the landing chopper. No way was I letting this scumbag slip through my fingers.

Taking down his men, I chased after Ron outside, without any weapon. But before I could reach him, he spun around, his arm snaking around my neck as he pressed his gun to my forehead. Panic surged through me, but I refused to let fear paralyse me.

Ayaan followed me out, but the moment he saw Ron pointing his gun at me, he froze on the spot, rifle levelled but unable to risk a shot with me as a human shield. Our eyes met, and I saw the silent communication pass between us. He wanted me to trust him, to believe that he had a plan to get us out of this.

"Back off," Ron barked at Ayaan, pressing the gun harder to my head. "Unless you want to be scraping up what's left of your agent."

My lungs burned, my vision hazing as the pressure on my throat intensified. I choked in his iron grip, seeing spots dance before my eyes. If Ayaan fired, he might be able to incapacitate Ron before the brute could put a bullet in me. It was my only chance, no matter how slim... But we wanted Ron alive. We can't shoot him.

Ron seemed to know exactly what I was thinking.

"Toss your piece over and let's be reasonable," he screamed again at Ayaan, dragging me backwards toward the chopper's lowered ramp.

Ayaan hesitated just a fraction too long. With a malicious chuckle, Ron pressed the hot barrel of the gun against my temple, daring Ayaan to make a move. Maybe if Ron took me along with him in the chopper, we wouldn't lose him yet. I could still have a plan to tackle this. Was that why Ayaan dropped his gun? Probably that was his plan too. But before we could act, a sharp crack split the air from behind me, and Ron's death-like grip on my neck loosened as he shoved me aside. I crashed to the ground, the impact sending a sharp pain through my head. What happened? My vision blurred as the world started spinning into darkness. All I could see was Ron's body collapsing mere feet away from me. He was shot dead. No, No, No! We needed him alive.

I blinked once, twice, struggling to make sense of the chaos around me. Who shot Ron? It wasn't Ayaan, for sure. Nothing registered beyond a dull, throbbing pain lancing through my skull, and then the darkness claimed me, and I knew no more.

CHAPTER 12 (PRICK TOO DEEP)

TRISHA

I jolted awake, the echo of gunshots and chopper blades still ringing in my ears. My heart hammered as fragmented memories flooded back—the firefight, chasing Ron, him using me as a human shield against Ayaan... And then a deafening boom, followed by searing pain as something slammed into me with brutal force. After that, only darkness remained.

Blinking rapidly, I took stock of my surroundings. The sterile walls and harsh lighting were clues enough—I was in a medical wing, tucked under a thin hospital blanket. A dull ache throbbed at the back of my skull, no doubt where I'd hit the ground.

But I was alive. Beaten and battered, yet somehow still breathing.

The door hissed open, and Sudesh, my team leader, strode in, his worn face creasing into a relieved smile. "Hey, you're awake. How are you feeling?"

I brushed aside his concern with an impatient wave. "What happened to Ron? Is he..."

"Dead," he replied after a beat, swallowing nervously. "But nothing's on our heads this time. It was the boss's call, so we can't exactly question that, can we?"

My blood ran cold at the implication.

"Who shot him?" I asked, already dreading Sudesh's response.

He shrugged, his expression hardening. "Krish."

My heart skipped a beat this time. Krish had shot Ron? Of course, he did. To save me. I can't believe it, though I understood his need to protect me. But capturing Ron alive was our primary objective to access the wider cartel network, however risky it seemed. Neutralising the target defeated the entire purpose of the op.

Unless...my thoughts circled back to those final frantic seconds, recalling the sadistic gleam in Ron's eyes as he dragged me toward the chopper. He'd been prepared to kill me without a second thought, seconds before his escape.

Had Krish seen that same scenario unfolding and taken the only action that could possibly save me? I squeezed my eyes shut, fighting back the sting of frustrated tears. I knew all too well what it meant to defy protocol in the heat of battle when a loved one's life hung in the balance.

What had he done? The repercussions would be severe once news of his unilateral decision reached his father's ears. The mission had failed without Ron, and so had our chance to gather crucial intelligence on the cartel. Was it all worth it? Only for me?

"Hey." Sudesh's gruff voice dragged me out of my spiral. "I know what you're thinking, but don't start beating yourself up about it just yet."

He settled onto the edge of the bed, fixing me with an earnest look. "Krish made a tough call out there, one that might very well cost him his career if the debrief goes sideways. But he did it to bring you home. And I'd bet every credit to my name he doesn't regret that choice for an even a second."

I opened my mouth to protest, to rage against the unfairness of it all, but Sudesh raised a hand to stop me.

"Just take a minute and be grateful you've got someone watching your back like that, yeah? That kind of loyalty is rare."

His words struck home with brutal clarity. Krish had sacrificed everything... for me. A strangled sob escaped my lips as Sudesh left the room. No matter the fallout, I wouldn't abandon Krish to face it alone. Not after he'd put my life above everything else.

And just as I made this resolve, my phone rang loudly next to the bed, and the caller ID flashing on the screen stole my breath away.

KRISH

Seated at the desk in our covert ops base, Phoenix Headquarters in Singapore, I focused on the mission reports, my jaw clenched so tightly that my temples throbbed. The room buzzed with activity as my team worked diligently to compile a report on today's mission, one that was meant to be a success but ended with an unexpected turn of events. The words blurred on the page as I forced myself to relive every painstaking detail of the operation. My mind drifted back to the chaotic scene at Ron's hideout.

With Trisha's tracking chip compromised by Max's men, dispatching Ayaan to rescue her became our most viable option. We relied on Ayaan's distinctive black beaded bracelet, equipped with a tracker, to locate them and pinpoint Ron's actual hideout. By the time my team and I arrived on the scene, the fight had escalated into a full-blown firefight between Ayaan, Trisha, and Ron's henchmen.

When Ron made his attempt to escape via chopper, everything shifted in an instant. I recalled the chopper landing, its blades slicing through the air with a deafening roar. My instincts screamed at me to take action, to explode the chopper and prevent Ron's escape. But then I saw him dragging Trisha towards the chopper, a gun pressed to her temple, and my priorities shifted entirely.

According to the plan, we were supposed to take the kingpin alive to extract vital information on the cartel's expansive network. But seeing Trisha's life hanging by a thread, I couldn't let protocol decide her fate. Without hesitation, I raised my gun and aimed at Ron, pulling the trigger.

My hand still burned from the recoil of the gun that dropped Ron like a sack of potatoes. In that split second, all remaining doubt had been dispelled. I knew the price, knew there would be consequences for deviating from the operation's primary objective, but in that moment, none of that mattered as Trisha's safety outweighed everything else.

She was receiving medical treatment for her head injury, still unconscious but stable, thanks to Ayaan's quick action, securing her after my shot. The thought of those agonising moments, not knowing if she'd survive, twisted my gut into fresh knots of dread. Only after she was airlifted with the emergency medical evacuation team did reality come crashing back in. We'd eliminated the heads of this particular cartel, but failed to extract crucial intel about the larger network.

I had made a choice, one driven by love and duty, to protect the woman I cared for above all else. Trisha was someone I couldn't bear to lose. And if given the chance, I would make the same decision again without hesitation.

Across the desk, Ayaan watched me impassively, giving me space to process everything. He understood me and the impossible choice I'd faced at the battleground today. Taking a slow breath, I turned to him. If anyone deserved answers first, it was the man who'd risked everything to get us this far.

"You're probably wondering why I took that shot instead of trying for a non-lethal takedown." My voice sounded flat, drained of emotion after wrestling with self-blame.

Ayaan merely arched an eyebrow in response.

"Yeah, I knew you would be," I replied to the unspoken question with a bitter chuckle. "Let's just say I don't have any regrets about putting that bastard in the ground after what he tried to pull."

My voice hardened as the memory resurfaced with double the intensity. "He was going to kill her right in front of us, then fly off to safety. And even if by some miracle she did make it, he'd just vanish into the ether with all the intel we needed to dismantle this drug cartel hierarchy."

I shook my head in disgust.

"So, you're damned right. I took the shot when I had it. Was it a violation of operational parameters? Sure. Did it put the entire mission objective at risk by eliminating our best chance at a bigger bust? Absolutely."

Ayaan continued to remain silent, just hearing me out as I continued.

"But Trisha is still alive because of it. And I'll make that call every single time if that's the price to keep my agents safe, no matter the consequences."

The silence stretched between us, thick enough to cut with a combat knife. Ayaan held my gaze for several heartbeats before giving a slow, solemn nod of understanding.

"I know you would," he said at last. "Which is why I'd follow you into literally any hellscape on this planet. Not many people have that kind of commitment. I know the protocols say completing the mission is our priority, but I, too, wouldn't let our agents lose their lives when we could save them in some way or the other, even if it means putting another few months of work into finding the intel that Ron could have provided us. I still believe saving Trisha was the right call."

I snorted at the praise, leaning back in my chair.

"Let's just hope the boss back in Austria, your father, sees it the same way when he debriefs us," he adds. "But don't worry, we'll handle it. Together. Like we always do."

There would be fallout; no doubt about it. Questions, second-guessing, and likely even disciplinary actions for going off-script in such an epic fashion. But as long as Trisha pulled through, as long as my team came home to fight another day, I could endure whatever hell rained down on me.

****

The medical staff informed me Trisha had already been dispatched to a safe house for recovery. Impatience gnawed at my gut as I made my way across the GLEN compound, desperate to see her after that harrowing brush with death.

I should have known she wouldn't rest once she regained consciousness. Stubborn as she was, of course, she'd already be back on her feet, likely packing her go-bag for the next high-risk deployment.

I keyed open the door to our safe house, the place where we lived together the last two weeks, and found Trisha in her room. She moved with her usual efficiency, stuffing gear and essentials into her bags. Just watching her in constant motion, safe and unharmed, filled me with overwhelming relief, a deep sigh escaping my lips as tension eased from my shoulders.

I crossed the threshold before she could turn and spot me, wanting nothing more than to feel her form against me, to affirm she was safe and real. Snaking my arms around her waist, I pulled her back flush against my chest and buried my face in the curve where her neck met her shoulder. The tension bled from my body as her familiar scent overwhelmed my senses.

This... this was what I'd risked everything to preserve. Not just her life, but her vitality, her spirit. For no idea how long, we remained locked in that embrace, my mouth tracing idle patterns across the warm skin left exposed by her loose shirt collar. Each breath brought her deeper into my body. As long as she was with me, everything was okay in my life.

But where I expected her hands to snake up and hold me in return, to sink into our embrace with the same bone-deep need, she remained unnaturally still and rigid. No welcoming caress, no murmurs of reassurance or affection. Nothing.

Furrowing my brow, I loosened my grip enough for her to turn and face me — only to be met with an expression of simmering anger rather than the relief I expected.

"What's wrong?" I breathed, confused by her sudden emotional distance.

"You shot Ron?" she growled in a tone usually reserved for hostile interrogations, not romantic reunions.

Ah, so that was the source of her ire. I almost smiled, relieved her anger stemmed from something as mundane as duty rather than a serious matter of the heart.

"You know why I had to," I replied, my tone hardening to match hers. "Your life was on the line, Trisha."

She regarded me with steely gaze. "So?"

The sharp rebuke caught me off guard. "So?" I echoed incredulously. "You wanted me to watch him pull the trigger on your head while I stood there like your life meant nothing?"

For the first time, I detected a flicker of uncertainty cross her features before the scowl returned. "What I mean to you isn't more important than the whole mission," she shot back. "We've vowed to take down the criminal world, not keep protecting each other at the expense of compromising those responsibilities. How many times are we going to be reminded of that?"

The muscles in my jaw ticked. She acted as though the choice to sacrifice her life for the mission should have been a simple matter of duty over personal attachment. As if she were just another asset to be risked.

"Even if I'm reminded a thousand times, I'll always choose your life over anything else on the line," I growled, unable to keep the edge from my tone as I grabbed her upper arms in a bruising grip. "That's what any man who loves you would do. That's what I would do because I love you, Trisha Chaudhary."

The moment the forbidden L-word slipped out, her expression crumpled. The word hung in the air between us, heavy with unspoken truths. I had never outright confessed my feelings for her, but in that moment, it felt necessary. She looked at me, tears glistening in her eyes, and I hoped that she understood.

I only wanted Trisha to understand how impossible it would be to just stand by and let her die for any mission. Not when she was my entire universe.

"Love?" Trisha's voice cracked on the word as she swiped at the tears from her cheeks. "You know that's not possible for people like us, right? It's forbidden."

I stepped closer, cradling her face in my palms as she tried to avert her gaze. "Why?" I demanded, tracing the sculpted line of her jaw until she met my intensity head-on. "Because we're on some never-ending crusade to save the world from the bad guys? Because you're just another agent under my command?"

She stiffened at the rhetorical questions. When she remained silent, I pressed harder. "Tell me why you think it's so damned forbidden for this to happen between us."

In a swift movement, she twisted free of my grip, putting space between us as she forcibly reassembled her mask of professionalism. "Because I don't love you, Krish," she bit out. "I can't."

I stared at her, dumbstruck. She... she didn't love me? After everything we'd been through together, all the life-or-death stakes we'd cheated side-by-side, she was rejecting the love I'd laid bare between us?

"You don't love me?" I echoed, my voice sounding distant and hollow even to my own ears. Anger surged in the wake of stunned disbelief. "Then what the hell was it between us these past few weeks? The days we've spent here showing how much we cared for each other, the kiss, the urge to go beyond the kiss… you're telling me that meant nothing?"

Trisha's expression remained stubbornly impassive. "Did I ever actually name it as love?" she countered with brutal honesty. "Did I ever tell you I wanted more than just... that?"

She didn't have to explain further. She never wanted something more serious and lasting. While I'd been falling deeper under her spell with every brush of skin and heated breath, she'd simply been living in the moment.

"I know it's not possible," she went on, her tone softening ever so slightly as she searched my face. "We might be attracted to each other, but we can never settle down, Krish. That's not on my agenda, not now, not ever. And if you can't understand or accept that..." Her voice trailed off, accompanied by a subtle shrug of her delicate shoulders. "It's time we put a stop to this before it gets too complicated. I don't want you harbouring false hopes that one day we can put this behind us, get married, and settle into some idyllic family dream."

The words sliced through me, infinitely sharper than any combat knife.

"These missions, this life—it gives me the adrenaline kick I've always craved," she continued in that same level tone that infuriated me. "I'm not ready to sacrifice that for anything. Not even love."

Love. She spoke the word with disdain, as if it were something distasteful she wanted no part of. At least, not where I was concerned.

I clenched my fists until the knuckles turned bloodless. Of course, I'd seen love blossoming in her warm smiles and gentle caresses, and like a fool, I'd misread all the signs she offered freely with no intention of following through.

When I finally trusted my voice not to betray the storm of hurt and anger raging within me, I spoke in a tone of forced calm. "If that's your decision, if you can't even see the possibility of us becoming more... then we should end this." I gestured vaguely between us, unable to give voice to the physical intimacies she was outright rejecting as meaningless. "Before it festers any further."

Her only reaction was the slightest dip of her chin, the barest nod of acknowledgement.

White-hot fury surged through me at her casual disregard for everything we could have built together—for the future I'd foolishly assumed was within our reach. I wanted to tell her so much more—to scold her, to put some sense into her, but words failed to form in my throat. I just wanted to end everything right there and leave, to hide myself from Trisha and not let her see how vulnerable she'd made me because of her admission at that moment.

"I wish you all the best in your missions to come, Agent Trisha." The formal title felt cold and impersonal on my lips as I spun on my heel, storming toward the door. I refused to look back, to let her see the storm ravaging my soul at that moment.

No more personal entanglements. This would never happen again, I silently vowed. I wouldn't let anyone exploit me emotionally hereon. And most importantly, never again would I make the mistake of giving my heart so freely, only to be rejected and discarded like trash. Trisha's words had pricked too deep this time to be healed anytime soon... or rather... to be healed in this lifetime.

CHAPTER 13 (NEVER AGAIN)

KRISH

As soon as I exited the cab in Austria, the gravity of my actions during the Singapore operation hit me like a heavy burden. No longer was I operating in the blind chaos of life-or-death decisions. Now, I would have to answer for my conduct—not just to the chain of command, but to the one man whose approval mattered the most—*my father*.

My father's summons had come through official channels, as expected, but the underlying message was crystal clear. It was time for me to face the ultimate debrief on why I had deviated so profoundly from the mission protocols. Why I had chosen to kill our prime asset—the drug cartel kingpin, Ron, in order to extract Trisha.

Exhaustion dragged at my every muscle as I made my way across the GLEN compound toward the central administration building. Ayaan had insisted on joining me, believing he could advocate for my perspective when facing my father's withering judgment. It was kind of him to even want to do so, but I knew it would prove fruitless in the end.

"They're going to bench you over this, you realise that, don't you?" he muttered under his breath as we approached the inner sanctum. "Probably suspend you on administrative leave until the heat cools off."

I shrugged, numb to the idea of any impending punishments. "If that's the call, so be it."

Ayaan shot me an appraising look from the corner of his eye. "And you're just... okay with that? Taking the hit without arguing your case?"

"What's there to argue?" The words tasted like ash on my tongue. "I knew the stakes going into it, knew there would be consequences for my choice. Doesn't change the fact that I'd make the same call again in a heartbeat, Ayaan. I don't care if he suspends me, but it's high time I tell him that the protocols need to be changed."

Ayaan said nothing more as we reached the inner doors leading to my father's office. As director-in-chief, Ayaan had already spoken to my father and debriefed him about what happened in Singapore, and now was the time to address my side. Dad wanted to speak with me privately.

I met Ayaan's worried frown with a curt nod, conveying both my understanding and my gratitude for his support. Whatever happened next, I would face it alone.

The door sealed shut behind me as I turned to face the lone figure settled behind the expansive desk, hands clasped together as he scrutinised me with narrowed eyes.

"This is the day I've feared my entire life," Dad began, the words said with bitter disappointment. "The day when my own son would willfully violate my organisation's most sacred protocols."

My throat bobbed with a swallow, but I held his cold stare in silence.

"I've already heard Director Shergill's account of the events," he went on, jaw clenching around the admission. "He tried to absolve you of any wrongdoing, to justify your reckless actions. But do you have anything to say in your own defence?"

The question hung between us, laden with subtext. This was the opening invitation to attempt rationalising my behaviour and wave off the disciplinary actions. Part of me wanted to seize it, to articulate every justification that had forced me to take the kill shot on Ron.

However, the part of me that felt tired and resigned couldn't come up with any good reasons. Especially when the truth was simply that I took the shot to save the woman I loved.

"No, Sir," I heard myself murmur. "I don't."

All the fight seemed to bleed out of my father then, as his shoulders sagged subtly. "Very well," he said in a tone carved from steel. "In that case, you are hereby suspended from all duties and operations of GLEN for no less than three months, effective immediately."

My jaw clenched hard, but I managed a terse nod of acknowledgment. The punishment was more than fair, possibly even lenient, compared to what could have been levied.

"Take this time to reflect long and hard," Dad went on. "Think carefully about the impact of letting personal relationships affect your decision-making in such important missions. Once you've gained some clarity, we can talk about what comes next for you."

"I don't regret my actions," I rasped through gritted teeth. "Nor do I regret the reasons behind them."

That, at last, seemed to rattle my father's legendary composure. He rocked back in his seat, eyebrows shooting upward in naked surprise. "You... don't regret putting the entire operation at risk?" he sputtered. "Risking years of work to dismantle the drug cartel, just for the sake of one asset?"

"Trisha is more than just some asset to be written off as an acceptable loss," I countered. "She is an integral part of the unit, a living, breathing member of my team whose life was in danger through no fault of her own."

I leaned forward, bracing my hands on the desk between us as I struggled to show the reason driving my decisions.

"As an integral part of this organisation, I believe I have the right to propose a change in our protocols. Our agents put their lives on the line in the field, facing injury, abduction, and even death. Yet, they never hesitate to carry out their missions. It should be our priority to protect them whenever possible, rather than allowing them to die before our eyes as if their lives mean nothing."

Dad listened in silence as I continued.

"If we fail to do this for them, who will? What sets GLEN apart from other organisations if we neglect to acknowledge and protect our assets when they're in trouble? If GLEN has the power to punish criminals, it should also have the power to safeguard its agents. If we can't do this, what separates us from the monsters we're trying to eliminate then? Our agents are our assets, Dad. We should be protecting them at all costs, not sacrificing them for some higher purpose."

To my surprise, my father listened without interruption. When I finished speaking, he nodded thoughtfully.

"That's..." Dad shook his head slowly. "That's a compelling point, Krish. One I'll need to... consider very carefully before I can offer any change like that. I'm not the only one who can make that kind of decision in protocols. But for now, you are benched for three months."

I accepted the decision with a sense of relief, grateful for the opportunity to step back from the chaos of my responsibilities. "I badly needed a break from all of this," I admitted. "So, thanks."

As I turned to leave, my father stopped me with one final question.

"One more thing before you're dismissed." His voice stopped me. "What about Agent Trisha? Don't tell me you're planning on chasing after her again during this newly granted leave?"

I felt my jaw flex as I shook my head, refusing to shy away from answering him.

"No more chasing after her, Dad," I replied with sincerity. "Trisha was an integral part of my life for a long time, that much is undeniable. But some people... some people are only meant to be with you for a short while. Until they've taught you whatever vital lesson you needed to evolve as a person. Trisha showed me that harbouring hopes of finding love in our profession is nothing but self-delusion," I continued. "I won't forget it. Never again."

I lifted my gaze then to meet his. Something flickered deep in Dad's eyes, the briefest glimmer of paternal remorse. He said nothing more, offering only the faintest of nods in response.

With my chest inexplicably tightening, I turned and strode for the exit without another word, blinking rapidly to disperse the hot tears blurring my vision. I would not weep, not in front of him or anybody. Not for Trisha, nor the hollowness left in her wake.

2 Years Later...

Mumbai. I returned to Mumbai again from Austria, where I had been for some paper trial work the last two weeks.

After my suspension from GLEN two years ago, I had spent those three months alone, licking my wounds from the Trisha ordeal. Those were dark days, but somehow, it helped me to toughen up my heart so it couldn't be crushed again. Ever.

Once I rejoined GLEN as a director, things finally seemed to be looking up. Dad and the committee had heeded our suggestions about preserving assets over sacrificing lives for intel. That policy change was a huge win, making all the struggles worthwhile.

Life in Austria was going smoothly as we successfully dismantled numerous criminal organisations worldwide. However, everything took a turn when Ayaan decided to visit India to celebrate his father Kailash Shergill's birthday. Ayaan ended up falling in love with Meher, the daughter of Pratap Walia, a political rival of the Shergills. While this was initially acceptable, Kailash uncle's sudden accident brought me to India to support Ayaan and uncover the truth behind the incident.

The Maze of suspicions, alliances, and potential targets began to unravel slowly, and as we delved deeper, it became apparent that a third party, likely a mafia group, was involved in Kailash uncle's accident, with the intention to frame Pratap Walia. Despite this revelation, Ayaan shocked us all by blackmailing Pratap Walia into agreeing to Meher's marriage with him. We all knew the Walias wouldn't agree to this, but when Ayaan Shergill, the king, played his moves on the chessboard, every other chess piece had to fall in its rightful place. So, true to his nature, Ayaan's plans always seemed to succeed.

Two days from now, my best friend would be tying the knot with his sweetheart. Ayaan had given me a crucial assignment: hire a personal bodyguard for his soon-to-be wife Meher. Despite the Walias' security detail—including Vishnu, Pratap's illegitimate son, and Meher's half-brother—she had still been abducted once before. Ayaan didn't trust them to protect his wife anymore.

He was right, of course. As the spouse of a GLEN director, Meher's safety would now be our responsibility. No more relying on the Walia family's inadequate measures. I would find her the best bodyguard money could buy and hand-pick a whole new security team myself if needed. Meher's well-being was about to become my top priority.

Having just returned to Mumbai, I wasted no time in briefing Ayaan about our plans to deal with the elusive Bat Gang, a group that had been targeting both the Shergills and the Walias for reasons yet unknown. The Shergill Mansion was bustling with activity as preparations for Ayaan's wedding were in full swing.

As I contemplated our next moves, Ayaan returned to the room, his mind already focused on a lot of things happening around him. "Krish, any progress with hiring Meher's personal bodyguards?" he inquired, and I presented the three best candidates I had selected.

However, Ayaan dismissed them all with a shake of his head. "None of these will suffice," he declared, his expression thoughtful. "In fact, I just realised we already have the perfect candidate for the job. I just had a conversation with Sudesh, and he informed me that she isn't currently assigned to any mission and is in India. This makes her a suitable candidate to take on Meher's security responsibility," Ayaan explained.

"Who are you talking about?" I asked, taken aback.

"Trisha Chaudhary," Ayaan replied. "You remember her, don't you?"

Trisha? My heart skipped a beat, flooding with her memories after two long years.

How could I forget? Two years ago, she had shattered me. I had worked relentlessly to rebuild myself, toughening my injured heart. Throwing myself into missions for GLEN had helped dull the ache. But even after all this time, just hearing her name ripped the emotional scars wide open again.

"Of course, I remember her," I managed to reply evenly, keeping my tone casual despite the roiling storm inside me. "But I don't understand. Why would she be a candidate for Meher's security?"

Ayaan sank on the couch next to me. "Sudesh informed me that Trisha recently completed a high-risk protection assignment in Europe. She has top-notch close combat skills and knows personal security protocols like the back of her hand."

He raised an eyebrow at me. "Plus, you knew her better than anyone. You can vouch for her abilities, right?"

I swallowed hard, feeling like I was trapped in some cruel joke. After everything Trisha had put me through, did Ayaan really expect me to welcome her back into my life, even in a professional capacity? Of course, he had no idea I had feelings for Trisha; otherwise, he wouldn't be bringing her back into my life after knowing how she had crushed my heart once.

Ayaan was right—I had witnessed Trisha's skills firsthand. She was a force to be reckoned with, and there were few people I trusted more to safeguard Meher's wellbeing.

Forcing my emotions down, I nodded slowly. "If Trisha is available and willing, then yes... she would be an ideal choice for this role."

"Excellent." Ayaan flashed that trademark confident grin. "Then you'll reach out and extend her the offer immediately."

"What?" I rose up. "I'll reach out to her?"

Ayaan shrugged.

"I've already called her tomorrow to meet us here in Shergill Mansion. But you know I'll be busy with the pre-wedding rituals, so you are the best person to talk to her and make sure she agrees to this."

He had already invited Trisha here tomorrow? I didn't know what to say further. But I couldn't refuse Ayaan, or he would be suspicious of my feelings for Trisha, the feelings that I'd buried long back and promised never to unearth again.

"Okay." I nodded weakly.

"Thanks, Krish." He rose and clapped me on the shoulder before heading for the door.

Once he was gone, I let out a shuddering breath, raking my hands through my hair. After two years of slowly piecing myself back together, Trisha was about to get thrown back into my world again.

Was I really ready to face the woman who had completely shattered me? I squeezed my eyes shut, clenching my fists as a fresh wave of anger, hurt, and longing washed over me.

For Meher's safety and Ayaan's sake, I had to be ready. No matter what it cost me emotionally, I would be professional.

The Krish she had known—the one who had foolishly allowed himself to become compromised, who was caught up in unrealistic dreams—no longer existed. The Krish she would meet again was now focused solely on his job, putting duty before anything else. Trisha and I might have a tangled past, but that didn't matter anymore.

CHAPTER 14 (A NEW BEGINNING)

TRISHA

I stepped through the ornate gates of the Shergill Mansion, my heart pounding. The lavish exterior was adorned with twinkling lights and colourful flower arrangements, all set for the Director's wedding. Ayaan Shergill was getting married to the Deputy CM's daughter, Meher Walia tomorrow.

Just yesterday, I received an unexpected call from Sudesh about this new assignment. After wrapping up my last mission—giving protection to a VIP in Europe, the last thing I expected was to be summoned back to Mumbai by Director Ayaan himself. And here I was, anxious and intrigued with what my next mission would be.

A smiling older man in a crisp suit greeted me.

"You must be Trisha. Ayaan and Kailash are expecting you."

"Hello, and you are?"

"Bhaskar, Kailash Shergill's assistant. You can call me Bhaskar uncle like everyone else does," he replied. "The Haldi ceremony hasn't begun yet. Ayaan will see you shortly in his study room. Right through there." He gestured towards an imposing wooden door.

I thanked him, trying to appear calm and professional despite my nerves. Taking a steadying breath, I turned the handle and entered the study.

The spacious room was dominated by a large leather chair, already occupied by someone whose back was turned towards me. Assuming it was Ayaan, I stood at stiff attention. "Hello, Director, it's nice to meet you again."

But when the chair swivelled around, I froze. It wasn't Ayaan in that seat.

It was Krish.

His eyes locked onto mine, and the world seemed to stop spinning. *Krish*—my... well, whatever we had been to each other two years ago—before I had foolishly thrown it all away and left him broken.

It had been two long years since our almost breakup, yet here we were, facing each other once more. I never anticipated this reunion, never wanted it. But fate had its own plans they said, and it seemed Krish and I were destined to cross paths again.

As Krish rose from his chair, I couldn't help but notice the change in him. He looked different than I remembered — older, more rugged and handsome in an effortlessly cool way. The warmth in his smile seemed to have faded, leaving behind a sombre expression. His expression was unreadable as he circled the desk and leaned back against it with his arms crossed. The silence between us stretched on, unnaturally cold and heavy with unspoken tension.

"Really?" he asked flatly when I didn't speak.

My mouth felt dry as a desert. What was he doing here? Of course, he and Ayaan were best friends, and since Ayaan was getting married, he had to be here too. But seeing Krish so unexpectedly unleashed a stampede of emotions I hadn't been prepared for.

I struggled to compose myself.

"Where is Director Ayaan? He called me here."

"Ayaan will be here shortly," Krish replied coolly. "And don't call him Director here. No one knows about our roles at GLEN."

I blinked in surprise at that revelation, but Krish continued without missing a beat. "Ayaan asked me to brief you on the role he wants you to take."

My heart stuttered as he explained further.

"Ayaan wants you to protect his would-be wife, Meher Walia, starting tomorrow," Krish explained, his words hanging heavily in the air. "You'll need to ensure her safety around the clock, which means you'll be staying here at the Shergill Mansion with us."

"Us?" I interrupted, confusion evident in my tone. "You... I mean... you're staying here too?"

"Unfortunately, yes. I'm stuck here with Ayaan until we uncover the identity of the gang that targeted Kailash uncle. The intel we have so far indicates that these people are dangerous, and both the Shergills and the Walias will need protection until we find them and understand their motives."

This was already more complicated than I could have imagined. Not only was I being forced to work with Ayaan Shergill again, but now there was Krish as well. It would be hard, especially after the way I had destroyed his heart and trust in me.

"Did you recommend me for this role to Ayaan?" I asked, almost accusingly.

Krish let out a mirthless chuckle. "If it were up to me, Miss Trisha Chaudhary, I would never recommend you to Ayaan. Not after our last conversation." His words felt like a slap. "So, no. This wasn't my idea at all."

I swallowed hard, taken aback by the cold fury simmering behind his eyes. This Krish was a far cry from the caring, affectionate man I had known. Understandably so, after how I had crushed him. But seeing the transformation up close pained me deeply.

"One last mission together," he stated flatly, all business now. "Are you in or out?"

I hesitated, knowing this could be emotionally devastating for me. For both of us. "Only if you don't mix up your feelings with the mission this time," I countered, my voice steadier than I felt.

Krish's jaw clenched, his expression darkening. "Who said I still feel for you? I've stopped looking for love in you a long time ago."

His harsh dismissal felt like a punch to the gut. Before I could muster a response, the study door swung open, and Ayaan strode in.

Pushing aside the storm of emotions, I straightened my spine and slipped into professional mode.

"Hello, Director," I greeted Ayaan with a smile.

"Hey Trisha, good to see you again. I'm sure Krish has briefed you already. So, are you in or out?" Ayaan asked.

I swallowed nervously but straightened my posture.

"I'm in, Sir."

"Good. Welcome back to the team, Agent Trisha," Ayaan replied, offering his hand for a handshake. I shook his hand, aware of Krish's gaze on me. I didn't know if I had made the right choice. But no matter what it cost me, I would be the flawless operative they needed. My past with Krish would never cloud my judgement again. I had made that mistake once before—I wouldn't be so foolish twice.

****

<u>A day after…</u>

After agreeing to this mission, I returned to Delhi yesterday to pack my belongings before moving into the Shergill Mansion in

Mumbai again to start my new job as Meher Shergill's bodyguard. That's why I missed Ayaan's wedding. This morning, I had settled into the guest room and ventured out to find Meher, wanting to properly introduce myself.

As I stepped out of my room, I nearly collided with someone – Krish himself. His damp hair and casual clothes made him look incredibly attractive, but exhaustion clouded his eyes. Despite my efforts to appear professional, I couldn't resist asking, "Didn't sleep well last night?"

Krish looked surprised by my concern.

"Didn't sleep at all. But don't worry, not because of you," he replied, with a mocking edge in his tone.

His jeering tone stung. Krish had never mocked me like this before. Lately, it felt like he took out all his frustrations on me at every opportunity. As he turned to leave, I blurted, "Would you be like this throughout now? Showing everyone around us that something is wrong between us?"

Krish stopped and slowly turned back to face me. With a stern expression, he closed the distance between us until we were merely a foot apart. Our bodies hadn't been this close in so long. And God knew how I wanted to slide my arms around him and embrace him. But I fisted my fingers to ensure I didn't make that mistake. Neither of us broke eye contact.

After a tense silence, Krish spoke, "Nothing was ever right between us in the past, Trisha. Whatever it was, you made it ugly for both of us. Why do you care now how coldly I behave with you in others' presence? Don't worry, I won't be like this in front of others. Even I don't want anybody here to know what a waste of time and feelings that was in the past."

He took another step forward, our noses almost touching, but he held my gaze as he continued, "Waste of time for you... and waste of feelings for me..."

Clenching his jaw as if trying to control his simmering anger, Krish stepped back and turned away, leaving without another glance.

My heart pounded in my chest. This was the meanest behaviour and harshest words Krish had ever directed at me. It definitely hurt. Krish's proximity reignited feelings I had buried deep within me. His words cut deep, reopening wounds I thought had healed. But despite the hurt, the familiar warmth of his presence stirred something inside me. As he walked away, a part of me yearned to reach out to him, to mend what was broken between us. But I knew better than to let my emotions cloud my judgment again.

Before I could dwell on it, I saw Meher, Ayaan's wife, enter the kitchen where Kailash Shergill was already cooking breakfast.

Deciding it was against professional ethics to think about Krish and his words right now, I made my way to the kitchen, intending to properly introduce myself to Meher Shergill as her appointed bodyguard.

****

It had been four days since I started working as Meher's bodyguard. She was a wonderful woman, and an excellent daughter and sister who was processing the fact that she had a half-brother — *Vishnu*. He had been staying at the Walia house, acting as her father's bodyguard and handling security for the family. Meher found out about this on her wedding night, and the next day she learned that her husband Ayaan had already known all along. The newlyweds had a fight, but the good husband that Ayaan was, he convinced her, and there was peace between them again, which I was glad for.

One thing I noticed through all this was that Krish's behaviour was cold and frustrated only towards me. With Ayaan, he was the same funny guy he used to be, and with Meher, too, he was slowly building rapport. But all that coldness and angry glares were restricted to me alone. Not that I minded, but it still hurt to see him behave so strangely with me every time. As if he didn't know me at all. As if we had never been close. As if he had never touched me. The mere thought of Krish's touch, knowing he was still a wall away from me, pricked me and made me toss in bed for hours.

It was night. Tomorrow, I had heard Ayaan and Krish planned to go to a club called "The Roost" to find someone called 'Raghav,' who apparently belonged to the Bat gang they were looking for. I wasn't yet an active part of that separate mission, which both my bosses were involved in, but I had been strictly instructed that Meher should not leave the house tomorrow when they were out. The task of protecting Meher and being her shadow was going great, except when she talked about Krish sometimes. I tried hard to keep my expressions neutral and not show that I was affected by him in any way. In his absence, it was easy to pretend I was unaffected, but living under the same roof as him made it hard for me to focus.

Unable to sleep, I got out of bed and made my way to the terrace to get some fresh air. But just as I entered, I saw Krish already there, smoking alone in the dark night.

As soon as I stepped onto the terrace, Krish noticed my presence. He took a long drag of his cigarette before speaking in a flat tone, "Couldn't sleep?"

"Yeah..." I replied, suddenly feeling self-conscious. Part of me wanted to turn around and leave, but I didn't want to appear rattled in front of him.

An awkward silence stretched between us. I could sense the tension radiating from Krish, like a raging storm desperately trying to be contained. Finally, I broke the quiet. "I'll just... get some air and go back inside."

Krish let out a harsh chuckle. "What, am I making you uncomfortable now? You used to be so comfortable around me once, Trisha."

His biting words stung, but I fired back. "Well, you certainly don't make it easy to be comfortable these days, Krish. The way you've been treating me..."

"Oh, like you've been perfect with me always?" He turned towards me, eyes blazing with sudden intensity. "After everything that happened between us, you think you have the right to expect better treatment from me?"

I felt tears prickling my eyes as a rush of memories assaulted me — memories of stolen glances, gentle caresses, deep kisses and whispered promises.

"I never intended to hurt you, Krish. You know that." My voice came out smaller than I intended.

In two strides, Krish closed the distance between us. He gripped my arms tightly, his face just inches from mine.

"Don't lie to me, now. Not again. You knew exactly what you were doing when you ripped my heart out."

His closeness was overwhelming. The scent of his cologne dredged up a torrent of longing I thought I had buried long ago. My lips parted involuntarily as my gaze dropped to his mouth.

Krish seemed to notice because his grip on my arms relaxed slightly. When our eyes met again, some of the anger had faded, replaced by an unmistakable heat.

We stood frozen like that, suspended in a heavy silence that seemed to reverberate with everything left unsaid between us. My heart pounded, whether from anger or impossible hope, I couldn't tell. Then Krish's hand lifted to delicately brush a stray lock of hair from my face. The gentle touch was like a spark, igniting the simmering tension into an inferno. Before I could overthink it, I surged forward and crushed my lips against his.

A strangled groan escaped Krish as he immediately responded with searing intensity. His arms encircled my waist, pulling me flush against his body as our mouths moved in frantic harmony. I tangled my fingers into his silky hair, deepening the kiss with every ounce of pent-up longing I'd harboured.

Our bodies pressed impossibly closer, seeking that achingly familiar friction. I could feel the hard planes of Krish's chest against my rapidly rising and falling chest. His hands roamed down my back in a blazing trail, caressing and kneading the supple curves, stroking the bare skin left exposed by my pulled-up top. I arched shamelessly into his touch, craving more of the delicious heat building between us.

Krish groaned against my lips as I tugged on his hair, tilting his head to ravage his mouth with deeper, hungrier kisses. Our tongues met in the most intoxicating way. I inhaled the spicy, masculine scent of him, feeling utterly drunk on his taste, his warmth, and the solid strength of his body moulded to mine. It felt like coming home after being lost for so long. It was all achingly familiar yet brand new at the same time. I never wanted this moment to end.

But eventually, the need for air became overwhelming. Krish tore his lips from mine, and we stood panting heavily, our ragged breaths mingling in the humid night air. His eyes bore into mine with a molten intensity that made my knees feel weak.

For a long moment, neither of us spoke. The world seemed to hold its breath as the weight of what had just happened stretched between us. Krish slowly lifted his hand to caress my flushed cheek, and I leaned instinctively into his touch, my eyelids fluttering closed.

Then, as if a spell had been broken, Krish abruptly stepped back, putting distance between our bodies again. I opened my eyes, only to witness the confusion and vulnerability swirling in his gaze.

"Krish..." I began uncertainly, my voice already husky from our passionate exchange.

He cut me off with a harsh shake of his head. "I'm not some toy for you to play with and discard whenever you feel like it, Agent Trisha." The use of my title, spat out like a curse, stung worse than a slap.

Krish's eyes raked over me with blatant accusation. "You think you can just seduce me, get whatever sick satisfaction you want, and then go back to treating me like I'm no one?"

I opened my mouth to protest, but he closed the distance between us again in two strides, gripping my arms in a punishing hold. "Do you enjoy doing that, Trisha?" he growled, his face mere inches from mine. "Stay the fuck away from me," he snarled.

The crude words felt like a punch to the gut, forcing the air from my lungs. Then, as abruptly as he had grabbed me, Krish shoved me away from him. I stumbled back a few steps, gasping for breath as he pinned me with a look of pure, undisguised loathing.

With that, Krish spun on his heel and stormed back inside, leaving me alone on the terrace. I could only clutch my arms around my torso as the hot sting of tears burned my eyes. Why the hell had I kissed him?

CHAPTER 15 (CHASING LOVE)

KRISH

<u>Next Day</u>

I paced restlessly around my room, my mind replaying the intense, unexpected kiss I'd shared with Trisha on the terrace last night. The memory of her soft lips crushed against mine, her fingers tugging at my hair, our bodies pressed together in a desperate, heated embrace — it all felt like a dream. Or rather, a torturous, tantalising nightmare I couldn't escape.

"Where the hell are my sunglasses?" I muttered, frantically patting my pockets. I needed a distraction, anything to get Trisha off my mind.

Just then, Ayaan strolled in, grinning from ear to ear. "Right here, genius." He plucked the sunglasses from my front shirt pocket and handed them to me.

I snatched them back, feeling my cheeks heat up. "I... I knew that."

Ayaan chuckled, his eyes gleaming with mischief as he leaned closer. "By the way, what happened to your lip? Got a little nibble there."

My fingers instinctively flew to my lower lip, and I winced at the tender soreness. Trisha's passionate bite mark was still there, a branded reminder of our encounter. I quickly glanced at the mirror, then back at Ayaan, hoping to play it off.

"Uhh, something must have bit me. I don't know."

"Something, huh?" Ayaan barked out a laugh. "Or should I say someone?"

I glowered at him, willing the blush to subside.

"I have no idea what you're talking about. And if you are here to waste my time, then get out. I've loads of work to do yet, all thanks to your silly plan of confronting Raghav alone in 'The Roost' pub."

"Why are you being cranky?" Ayaan mocked.

"I'm not being cranky," I muttered, cutting off Ayaan mid-sentence. "In fact, why are you in my room? Why aren't you bothering your wife today?"

Ayaan chuckled, plopping down on the sofa. "She's busy with Dad in the kitchen. She has no time for me for now."

"So, you mean I'm your backup for timepass?"

Ayaan chuckled.

"Something is definitely wrong with you, buddy. You got mood swings?"

I rolled my eyes. "Can we just focus on the plan for your 'Roost encounter' with Raghav?"

"Alright, alright." Ayaan held up his hands in surrender, though the amusement never left his expression. "So, about confronting Raghav at The Roost..."

As Ayaan outlined the details of our mission, I found it increasingly difficult to concentrate. All I could think about was the way Trisha had kissed me, the desperate heat and hunger in her touch. I'd never expected her to initiate something so passionate, so unrestrained. It had caught me completely off guard.

"Back to earth, Krish!" Ayaan's voice suddenly snapped me back to the present. "You still with me?"

"Huh? Oh, yeah, sorry." I avoided looking at him because I knew the moment my friend would look into my eyes, he would know I'd fallen in love. I still was in love. *With Trisha.* No matter how much I denied that, even to myself.

"As I was saying," Ayaan continued, "we need a team on standby in case things go south with Raghav. Local police too. What do you think?"

I nodded firmly. "Absolutely. They'll be ready."

Ayaan rubbed his palms in excitement. "Excellent. Now, let's go over the plan one more time..."

As the discussion continued, the thoughts of our kiss haunted my mind again. That kiss had shattered the carefully constructed walls I'd built to keep her out. I shook my head, trying to focus on the task at hand. But the memory of Trisha's lips, her touch, her taste — it was all I could think about.

Just as Ayaan and I were going over the mission plan one more time, there was a knock at the door.

"Come in," Ayaan called out.

Trisha entered, her gaze briefly meeting mine before she turned to Ayaan. "Boss, I've shifted my stuff to the other guest room downstairs. That's the key to my previous room." She handed the keys to Ayaan.

I felt a pang of confusion. She had changed rooms? Moved downstairs?

"Great," Ayaan said. "I hope you're comfortable in your new room. Let me know if there's anything else."

Trisha nodded. Ayaan's phone rang, and he quickly excused us and walked out of the room to answer. Trisha turned to leave, but I couldn't stop myself from speaking up.

"You changed the room?" I asked, trying to keep my voice even. "Not interested in even sharing a wall between us now?"

Trisha paused, crossing her arms as she faced me. "Isn't that what you asked me to do? To stay the fuck away from you?"

Her words struck a chord, and I was suddenly reminded of the cruel, bitter things I'd said to her last night after our heated kiss. I opened my mouth, but no words came out.

"I'm just obeying the Director's orders," Trisha continued, her tone clipped. She turned to leave, but I reacted instinctively, reaching out to grab her arm and whirl her back around, pinning her against the door.

"You're obeying the orders, but you're also raising suspicion in the eyes of the people around," I warned, my face mere inches from hers. "I don't want Ayaan or Meher to know what we had between us, Trisha." I paused, my gaze boring into hers. "Or rather, what I thought we had, but you never cared."

Trisha's eyes darkened with the same intensity as her voice.

"I shifted my room because Meher insisted," she replied. "The shower in my room wasn't working, and she urged me to move downstairs. I agreed, thinking that was the best I could do to follow your orders of staying away from you as much as possible, Krish." She tilted her head slightly. "But why do I sense you're not happy with it? Isn't this what you wanted—for me to stay away?"

I was speechless again, cursing my own conflicting emotions. Trisha's gaze dropped to my lips, where the faint bruise from her passionate bite last night was still visible. She quickly averted her eyes, meeting mine again.

"*Your* behaviour can make it obvious to them that something is wrong between us, not mine," she said. "You need to keep a check on your feelings, Krish. Because I've learned to do that a long time ago."

With that, Trisha gently pushed me away and walked out, leaving me perplexed. What did she mean by that? Did it mean she was hiding her feelings from me?

I ran a hand through my hair, frustrated. Everything about Trisha and our relationship was so goddamn complicated. One moment, I couldn't stand to be around her; the next, I was craving her touch, her kisses, her warmth. And now, she was the one maintaining a distance, following my own orders to stay away.

"Tough day!" Ayaan's voice broke through my thoughts. He had returned, a sympathetic look on his face as he scrolled through his phone.

I let out a humourless chuckle. "You have no idea."

I was sure he didn't hear anything that Trisha and I spoke.

Ayaan clapped me on the back. "Well, at least we've got a plan in place for 'The Roost'. Hopefully, we can get some answers from Raghav and move this whole Bat gang investigation forward."

I nodded, grateful for the change in subject. "Yeah, let's hope so. The sooner we can wrap this up, the better."

As Ayaan delved back into the mission details, I tried to focus, but my mind kept drifting back to Trisha's parting words. Had she truly learned to control her feelings for me? And if so, did that mean she cared about what we once had?

The thought filled me with a strange relief. But I pushed it aside, knowing I needed to have my head in the upcoming mission.

****

A week later

It had been a busy week since Ayaan's confrontation with Raghav at The Roost. The revelations and the interconnected pasts about the Bat Mafia's true leader, a man whom we termed as 'The Bishop', had created a tense atmosphere in the Shergill Mansion. And the only person who was affected the most by these revelations was my friend, Ayaan Shergill. But I knew Ayaan would overcome this with the support of Meher and Kailash uncle. I would be there for him as well, no matter what.

As I searched for Meher to brief her on the security arrangements for the upcoming private event organised by Pratap Walia's NEP party, I spotted Trisha hurrying out of her room, phone pressed to her ear.

"Yug, what time did you land?" she asked, her voice held a hint of excitement I hadn't heard from her in a long time. "I've texted you the address. I'll be there in fifteen minutes. Can't wait to see you, darling."

Darling? My jaw clenched as I listened to the sweet endearment roll off her tongue. Who the hell was this 'Yug' she was meeting?

Trisha must have sensed my presence because she suddenly turned around, her eyes locking with mine. For a brief moment, she hesitated, then quickly averted her gaze and continued on her way.

Before I could intervene, Trisha reached Meher, who was in the living room.

"Meher, I'll be back in an hour. Remember, I had told you yesterday about going out to meet someone?"

"Yes, yes, I remember," Meher replied. "You take your time, and since Ayaan is at home, I'm not going anywhere. You can enjoy the free time you rarely get."

Trisha thanked her and hurried out the door. I approached Meher, frowning.

"Why did you let her go? She's here to protect you, not run off and enjoy herself."

Meher frowned back at me.

"Come on, Krish. I know she's on duty, but she doesn't need to be when I'm at home. And she had told me about this special person she had to meet today. It's fine. She has a life too."

I felt my disappointment and curiosity swelling in equal measure. Who was this 'special person' in Trisha's life? I quickly made an excuse to Meher about a meeting I had to attend and rushed out the door, following Trisha as she got into a hired cab and left the Shergill Mansion.

I knew it was completely unprofessional of me to do this, but I couldn't help it. Anything related to Trisha had become my business, whether she liked it or not. I started my car and pulled out, careful to keep a safe distance as I tailed her cab through the busy streets of Mumbai.

After a short drive, Trisha's cab pulled up in front of a small café. I parked a few blocks away and watched as she hurried out of the cab, a smile lighting up her face. A few minutes later, a young man emerged from the café and enveloped Trisha in a warm hug. I gripped the steering wheel, my knuckles turning white as I observed their intimate interaction.

They soon broke apart, and the man—presumably this 'Yug'—took Trisha's hand, leading her back into the café. I sat there, warring with the urge to storm in and confront them. But what right did I have? Trisha had made it clear that she had no feelings for me, and she would never settle down with me either.

Yet the thought of her being with someone else, of her sharing those tender moments with another man, made my blood boil. Just a week ago, she had kissed me like she wanted me back in her life, and I had pushed her away, told her to stay the fuck away from me. And today, she is meeting someone else who was already so close to her.

I had no claim on her, no right to feel this way. But the heart wants what the heart wants, and mine still craved Trisha in a way I couldn't ignore.

I sat there for what felt like an eternity, watching the cafe, watching the door, waiting for Trisha to emerge, a cigarette dangling between my fingers as I struggled to ease the tension and anger roiling inside me. When she finally did, nearly an hour later, she was beaming. The man, Yug, accompanied her, and I couldn't resist the urge to get out of the car and confront them. Crushing my cigarette under my heel, I approached the pair.

"So? We are meeting again soon, right?" Yug asked Trisha, a hopeful glint in his voice. "Now that we're in Mumbai, we should keep seeing each other."

"Of course, we will," Trisha replied, a smile lighting up her face.

"I'll drop you then?" Yug offered.

"Oh, no. I don't want you to worry," Trisha demurred.

"But then how will you go?" Yug pressed.

"She'll go with me," I interjected, joining their conversation.

Yug looked surprised at my intrusion, but Trisha's expression told me she had known I was there the whole time. Of course, she had—she was a spy, after all, with eyes everywhere.

"And who are you?" Yug asked, glancing between Trisha and myself.

Trisha quickly made the introductions. "He's my boss, Krish. And Krish, this is Yug."

Yug. That name again. I clenched my jaw, waiting for Trisha to elaborate on who exactly this Yug was to her. But she remained infuriatingly tight-lipped.

"Yug... who?" I practically snapped, needing to know.

Yug, sensing the tension, interrupted.

"Alright, Trishi, you carry on then. I'll see you soon."

Trishi? He had the audacity to call her by some sickeningly sweet endearment? My blood boiled as I watched Yug lean in and press a kiss to Trisha's cheek, murmuring, "Love you."

"Love you more," Trisha replied, and I damn near had a heart attack. She could say those words so easily to this Yug, when she had never said them to me?

I somehow managed to contain my anger and jealousy until Yug had gotten into his car and driven off. The moment he was gone, I grabbed Trisha by the arms, turning her to face me.

"So, he's the one because of whom you couldn't reciprocate my feelings?" I demanded, my grip tightening. "Or did he just recently enter your life, and you changed your ideologies about giving relationships and commitment a chance?"

I pulled her closer, our bodies nearly flush.

"And if that's the case, then how could you just choose someone else? Didn't you think about me even for a moment? You knew how much I loved you, Trisha, and yet you didn't come back to me?"

I poured out all my pent-up feelings, but Trisha remained infuriatingly silent. When I finally paused, she shrugged off my hold and crossed her arms defensively.

"Yug is my nephew," she stated simply.

My anger suddenly cooled down, like someone had just thrown a bucket of ice water on me. *Nephew?* I looked Trisha up and down, making sure I heard correctly.

"Nephew? How is that possible? He looks almost your age," I questioned.

Trisha rolled her eyes. "So? His mother, my cousin sister, was almost my mother's age. Yug is her son, my nephew."

She fixed me with a stern gaze. "And tell me, Krish, how does it even matter to you what Yug or any other man in my life means to me? Didn't you tell me the other day that you have no more feelings for me? To leave you alone, to stay away from you? So why are you interfering in my life now? Or should I say, you lied to me that time — that I don't mean anything to you anymore. Because you are clearly overreacting now?"

I was speechless as she continued.

"When I left the Shergill Mansion, I saw your car following me. If I wanted, I would have stopped right then and confronted you. But I wanted to see how far you'd go to interfere in my personal matters. That's why I didn't stop you. I continued with my plans and met Yug here."

I was dumbfounded as she unleashed her rant.

"You say you don't have feelings for me, then why did you follow me? Stalk me? Jealousy and insecurity are written all over your face, Krish. I'm sure even Yug could see that. You behaved like you have rights over me, and then you have the audacity to ask me to stay away? Why these double standards? You were burning in anger when Yug kissed my cheek."

"Of course, I would burn with anger and jealousy, seeing him touch you. No one is supposed to touch you, Trisha. No one but..." I trailed off, unable to finish the sentence.

Trisha and I both went silent, the implication of my words hanging heavily in the air. I was the first to break the trance, banging my fist against the pillar beside us in frustration.

"Let's go," I muttered, turning to head to my car, but Trisha grabbed my elbow, stopping me and pinning me to the pillar.

"Tell me honestly, Krish. Do you still love me?" she asked, her gaze unwavering.

I stared at her blankly, contemplating my response. "What would you do, even if I gave you an honest reply, Trisha?"

Her expression faltered, and I let out a sardonic smirk.

"See, you don't have an answer to that, do you? That's why I'm not answerable to you, either, Trisha."

With that, I shrugged off her hold and walked away to my car, needing to put some distance between us. As I climbed into the driver's seat, I couldn't help but glance back at Trisha, standing there alone, her beautiful face etched with a mix of confusion and... regret?

I clenched the steering wheel, my knuckles turning white. Why did this woman have such a hold over me, even after all this time? Even after I had tried so hard to push her away, to convince myself that I no longer cared?

The truth was, I was still utterly, hopelessly in love with Trisha. And the thought of her moving on, of her finding happiness with someone else — even if that someone was just her nephew — it tore me apart inside.

But what right did I have to demand her affection, her loyalty, when I had so cruelly rejected her in the last week when she kissed? With a resigned sigh, I started the car. I knew I couldn't avoid Trisha, not when we were both a part of the Shergill household. But I would have to find a way to keep my distance, to guard my heart against the temptation of her presence. Because if I let myself fall for her again, I knew I might not survive the heartbreak a second time around.

CHAPTER 16 (SAFE HEAVEN)

TRISHA

The next evening, we were getting ready to attend the event—a party hosted by the NEP party. Since both the Shergills and the Walias were invited, it was inevitable that Krish and I would be there too.

I watched Krish conversing animatedly with Ayaan in the living room. They were discussing the security arrangements for both families, especially now that they knew who our enemy was—Raghav and Ayaan's real father, the Bat gang leader, Tej Khurana. It was clear that we needed to be more cautious than ever before.

Yesterday, when Krish followed me to the café where I'd been to meet Yug, it had struck a chord deep within me, igniting a flicker of hope that perhaps his feelings for me had never truly faded. But then, his parting question had doused that hope, leaving me uncertain again.

He was right to ask me what I would do if he admitted he still loved me. I honestly didn't know. Part of me longed to throw myself into his arms, to finally give in to the consuming desire that had always burned between us. But another part—the logical part—knew that opening myself up to that kind of vulnerability again could mess everything up for him. I was ready to lose anything but not what Krish had built all these years with his hard work.

That is why compartmentalising my feelings for Krish and focusing solely on my duties was a must. But seeing him, hearing the raw emotion in his voice, it had all come rushing back, threatening to overwhelm me.

Even now I couldn't help but admire him. His sharp focus on the subject matter, his passion for work, and his selfless friendship with Ayaan Shergill—it was all so captivating. Today, Krish was dressed in a crisp white shirt and blue jeans, looking more attractive than ever. And to top it off, he had just gotten a fresh haircut, adding to his charm and appeal. His lively movements, the way his muscles flexed beneath his shirt, ignited a physical longing within me—a desire to reach out and touch him. I wanted to trace the strong lines of his jaw, to feel the warmth of his skin beneath my fingertips, to press my lips against the curve of his neck, and to trace the firm lines of his biceps with my tongue. Yet, I pushed these desires aside, just as I had been doing for the past two years.

Krish may not have deserved my love, but he certainly deserved an apology from me, at the very least. I owed him an apology for causing him pain in the past and for being the source of his continued anguish even today. It was clear that Krish had not moved on from me. He was tirelessly building walls between us because I was not ready to acknowledge my feelings for him. Offering an apology could, at the very least, provide him with some solace, help him find closure, and allow him to move forward. Most importantly, it would offer me some comfort, knowing that I could give him something, even if it wasn't my heart.

As I walked past them, lost in my thoughts, and keeping my gaze fixed on Krish, I suddenly collided with someone.

"Oh, I'm so sorry!" I exclaimed, my cheeks flushing with embarrassment as I realised it was Meher.

Meher looked at me curiously, her eyes filled with understanding as she glanced between me and Krish, who was still oblivious of my admiration.

"Are you okay, Trisha? You seem a bit distracted," she remarked.

I quickly composed myself, masking my inner turmoil with a forced smile. "Yes, I'm fine. Just lost in some thoughts," I replied, hoping she wouldn't probe further.

Thankfully, Meher didn't press the matter and excused herself to get ready for the event. Glancing back at Krish, I quickly pulled out my phone and typed out a message, needing to reach out to him in some way, even if I couldn't find the courage to do it in person. Taking a deep breath, I hit send and hurried off to my room to get ready for tonight's event.

KRISH

As Ayaan and I finalised the last details of our security plans for tonight's event, my phone buzzed in my pocket. Ignoring the distraction, I continued speaking, but curiosity gnawed at me. And I couldn't resist any longer and checked the notification.

Glancing at the screen, I saw a message from Trisha: "I'm sorry."

My heart skipped a beat. Why was Trisha apologising? I quickly scanned the room to see if she was around, ensuring Ayaan hadn't noticed my distraction, before returning the phone to the table.

Questions flooded my mind. Was Trisha here? Yesterday, when I followed her and even admitted to feeling jealous upon seeing her with another man (Yug), I realised that I had made a huge mistake by revealing to Trisha that my feelings for her still lingered. But what prompted her sudden apology now? In fact, I should be apologising for still interfering in her personal life. Shaking off my thoughts, I refocused on the conversation with Ayaan. I would deal with Trisha's apology later. Right now, we had a job to do.

****

As I approached the car late evening, ready to leave for the event, my gaze immediately locked onto Trisha, who was already seated in the front passenger seat, looking absolutely stunning in a tight black button-down shirt that hugged her curves in all the right places, sleeves rolled up to her elbows. She had paired it with a pair of equally form-fitting black jeans, a gun holster strapped snugly around her waist.

Even after all this time, Trisha had the power to make my pulse race and my body harden with wanton desire. That woman could dress up a gunny sack and still look like a goddess.

I had intended to talk to her about the apologetic text message she had sent me the today, but as I approached the car, Meher had already climbed into the backseat. With Ayaan sure to occupy the spot next to his wife, the only place left for me was the driver's seat.

Not that I was complaining. Any opportunity to be near Trisha, even if it meant maintaining a professional distance, was better than nothing.

Just as I was about to slide into the driver's seat, Ayaan called out to me.

"Krish, you're coming with Dad and Bhaskar uncle in their car, right?"

I quickly formulated an excuse.

"One guard is needed in that car, so Alex will be escorting them. I'll be driving this one."

Ayaan shrugged, but I caught a subtle glimmer of suspicion in his eyes as I settled behind the wheel. I couldn't blame him — my sudden insistence on driving this particular car was hardly inconspicuous. I gestured for Alex to drive with the elders, started the engine, and pulled out.

I glanced at Trisha from the corner of my eye. She was gazing out the window, her expression unreadable. I desperately wanted to broach

the subject of the apologetic text she had sent me, to understand where her head and her heart were at. But the presence of Ayaan and Meher in the backseat had effectively thwarted any chance of a private conversation. Worse still, Ayaan and Meher seemed to be in a passionate mood after some time, their stolen kisses filling the car. I couldn't help but glance at Trisha from the corner of my eye, wondering how she was coping with the intimate display. She had witnessed their kiss, too, and the look in her eyes told me that she was reminded of our scorching kisses. Trisha's eyes sparkled as she met my gaze, but she quickly looked away, not letting that spark blaze. I immediately cleared my throat to interrupt Ayaan and Meher's cosy act behind.

"Guys, you know I don't mind what you're doing in the backseat, but we have another lady here amongst us," I quipped, unable to resist the urge to break the tension.

"I don't mind that either. Please don't speak on my behalf," Trisha replied, almost scolding me for interrupting them.

Ayaan pulled away from Meher, grinning at me through the rearview mirror. "See, the lady doesn't mind," he said, nodding towards Trisha. "But why do you look so uncomfortable, Krish?"

I gripped the steering wheel tighter, trying to tamp down the flicker of jealousy that had ignited within me.

"Well, that's because you get to sit in the backseat, and I don't," I retorted.

"I never said I wanted to sit here. I was okay with driving. It was you who said you wanted to drive," Ayaan countered.

"Well, that's because Meher had already taken the backseat," I argued. The truth was, I wanted sit next to Trisha, to bask in her presence, even if I couldn't bring myself to touch her.

Ayaan's tone took on a teasing lilt. "Or... was it because Trisha had already taken the front passenger seat? And you thought of impressing her with your driving skills?"

I glowered at him through the rearview mirror, feeling Trisha's gaze dart towards me before she quickly looked away, a faint blush tinging her cheeks. Meher noticed the exchange, nudging Ayaan with a knowing smile.

Desperate to change the subject, I announced, "We're approaching the venue."

As I pulled up to the curb, I took a deep, steadying breath. This was going to be a long, difficult evening, with Trisha's intoxicating presence mere inches away, yet so unbearably out of reach.

I just hoped I could keep my emotions in check and maintain my professionalism. Because the last thing I needed was for my heart to betray me in front of everyone.

****

A while later...

As Ayaan and I had feared, the NEP party event turned out to be a trap—a ploy orchestrated by Tej Khurana to reveal himself to Ayaan and demand that he abandon the Shergills and Walias to join his criminal empire instead.

The nerve of that man! When Ayaan refused, outright rejecting Tej's twisted demands, he managed to target a short circuit, plunging the Shergill Mansion into darkness.

I had driven Meher, Kailash uncle and Trisha back from the event to the mansion, and we had just got out of the car when the short circuit happened at the monitoring room of the Ayaan's home, and the power went out. Our security teams immediately sprang into action, working to secure the premises and ensure there were no further risks to the family's safety.

Ayaan and I, however, had a contingency plan in place—a safe house located in the outskirts of Mumbai, roughly 30 kilometres from the city. It was one of the many secure facilities maintained by GLEN, our organisation, for situations just like this.

As the teams handled the situation at the mansion, I remained inside, frantically trying to recover any salvageable data and devices from the monitoring room. The heat and smoke from the short circuit had taken a toll, giving bruises to my arm as I fought to extinguish the small flames consuming the critical hardware.

I coughed incessantly, the harsh fumes stinging my lungs, when a familiar touch suddenly grasped my hand, pulling me away from the chaos. Blinking through the haze, I found Trisha at my side, her eyes filled with a mix of worry and concern. She handed me a water bottle, and I immediately gulped some water down, to soothe my raw throat.

"Thanks."

"Better?" Trisha asked, taking the bottle back, her gaze sweeping over me. I acknowledged with a nod. "The team is handling the stuff. Why are you still in there? And without a mask, no less. How would the smoke not affect you? Stop being so careless, Krish."

She obviously cared for my well-being. I'd rarely seen Trisha's fiercely protective side for me, and it felt good.

"Why did you send me that text?" I finally asked, ignoring the timing.

Trisha's eyes softened.

"We can talk about that later. Right now, you need to tend to these bruises. Come on, let's get you checked out, Director."

Before I could protest, she was leading me away from the billowing smoke, guiding me towards the waiting medical team. I knew I should have argued and insisted on staying to oversee the operation, but in that moment, I was utterly powerless to resist Trisha's care and concern.

Once the medics had tended to my minor injuries, Trisha and I joined Ayaan, Meher, and Kailash uncle in preparing to leave for the safe house. As I settled behind the wheel again, with Trisha sliding into the passenger seat beside me, I couldn't help smiling back at her. I wished things between us were not bitter. But I knew that was a foolish hope. The pull I felt towards Trisha was as strong as ever, the desire to reach out and touch her, to simply be near her, nearly overwhelming. Yet I knew I couldn't act on those impulses until she didn't want the same. So, I kept my focus firmly on the road ahead, determined to get us to the safe house first. For now, the priority was the safety of the Shergill family, and I couldn't afford to let my own personal demons distract me from that.

****

We arrived at the safe house. It had a cosy living room, a basic kitchenette, and two bedrooms on the ground level, with a terrace and a small gym room situated upstairs. My team quickly secured the premises, and we all settled inside. Kailash and Bhaskar uncle took one of the bedrooms, while Ayaan insisted that Trisha and Meher take the other, leaving Ayaan and me to bunk down on the small living room couch.

But just as Ayaan said that, Trisha spoke up. "You and Meher take the bedroom. Krish and I will be fine here on the couch."

I was stunned, my gaze immediately snapping to Trisha. Was she truly suggesting that we share the sofa? The prospect thrilled me.

Ayaan seemed equally perplexed, hesitating to accept Trisha's offer. "But—"

"Trisha is just doing her job, buddy," I interjected, surprising even myself with my eagerness to back up her proposal.

Trisha shot me a grateful look before addressing Ayaan again. "The Boss agrees. Sofa it is for me and him."

With some reluctance, Ayaan and Meher finally agreed, retiring to the bedroom and leaving Trisha and me alone in the small living area.

An awkward silence settled between us as we busied ourselves with arranging the couch for the night. As I brewed the coffee in the small kitchenette next to the living room, I couldn't help but steal glances at Trisha. She had just unbuckled her gun holster and put it aside. She then let her hair down from the ponytail and unleashed her beautiful curls. I was instantly mesmerised. Trisha made her way to the washroom, and emerged a few minutes later, dabbing her face to alleviate any signs of exhaustion. Unable to resist, I offered her a freshly brewed cup of coffee.

"Umm. I missed your coffee," she said, sipping the coffee, her eyes widening as if surprised by her own words. The memory of our time in Singapore flooded back—the mornings we spent together, me brewing the perfect cup of coffee for us, adding that extra touch of cocoa powder on top. Those were some of the happiest moments I'd ever experienced.

Trisha quickly averted her eyes, trying to walk away, but I gently held her hand, stopping her.

"What else did you miss?" I asked, my heart racing.

The pain on Trisha's face was noticeable, but she hid it effectively. She looked down, and I took the opportunity to continue. "At least tell me why you apologised, so I can rest in peace."

"Stop talking like that, Krish. I don't like it," she said, hitting my chest gently, her eyes now filled with anger.

"Your list of *'don't like'* is getting longer day by day," I replied with a smirk. "You don't like me following you, you don't like me showing affection towards you, you don't like me getting close to you, and most importantly, the first one on the list... you don't like me at all."

"Did I ever say that?" she frowned. "Stop putting words in my mouth."

"Not my fault. I like feeding you," I winked, the tension between us heightened. Realising the double meaning of my words, I quickly clarified, "I mean, there were times when I fed you food in Singapore. Remember?"

Trisha rolled her eyes. "I should have let you and Ayaan sleep together tonight. I was better with Meher inside."

She sipped her coffee and settled down on the couch, pretending to frown. I sat down beside her, snatching the coffee mug from her hand, and taking a sip. She didn't mind.

"So? Why did you send that text to me?" I asked again, the seriousness returning to her expression.

"I had to apologise to you for everything, right?" she queried. "I broke your heart."

"And you think an apology can fix it?

"You'll get the closure you need, at least. Move on, Krish," she argued.

"Have you?" I probed, putting the coffee mug away.

"Krish, don't do this. Please. You know we two have no future together."

"Says who?"

"Your father," she blurted out, and my heart skipped a beat.

My father! What did my father have to do with this? The way Trisha's own expression changed, it was clear that she hadn't meant to reveal   that information. There was more to this than she was letting on, and I was determined to get to the bottom of it.

CHAPTER 17 (IN YOUR ARMS)

TRISHA

"My father?" Krish asked, sounding confused as to why I had brought up his name. I wasn't prepared to answer his question or dig up the old graves that I thought had been buried for good.

"I'm sleepy," I lied, trying to get up, but Krish gripped my hand, preventing me from leaving.

"What are you hiding?" he demanded.

"Nothing," I replied, but he wasn't convinced.

"You wouldn't have brought my father into this conversation for nothing, Trisha. Why do I sense you're hiding something important from me?"

Just like that, my eyes welled up with tears. I felt weak and vulnerable, emotions I had fought hard to suppress resurfacing. I didn't want to cry, but Krish pulled me close to him.

"Trisha, if you don't speak up now, we might never get over this. Look at me... I haven't been able to move on from you, wondering what made you reject feelings despite seeing those same feelings in your eyes throughout our time together. I've thought about it every single day for the last two years. If you don't tell me what the real matter is, I'll go crazy trying to connect these dots myself. Is that what you want?"

I shook my head, brushing off his words. "I don't want to create a rift or misunderstanding between you and your father, Krish. So, just let it go. We don't have to talk about this. I know you love me, you still do, but that doesn't change the fact that we still have no future together."

Anger flashed in Krish's eyes as he interrupted me.

"It is we who will decide if there is a future for us or not. But the way I'm seeing this now, I'm confident Dad has something to do with your rejection of my feelings all this time, Trisha. Speak up."

I remained adamant, unwilling to share the truth. Krish grew increasingly frustrated.

"Fine, let me ask him directly, then." He took his phone out of his jeans pocket and was about to dial his father's number when I stopped him, snatching the phone away and putting it aside.

"Don't get him into this now," I pleaded.

"Why?" Krish asked in a hushed voice, though I could sense he was barely containing his urge to shout and scream at me.

"Because he is right. Your father is justified in reminding us of our professional duties. He loves you, Krish. And all he wants is to see you at the level where he is today. And that's only possible if you stay committed to your role and don't deviate from it because of a woman like me."

Krish grabbed my arms, his jaw clenched as he stressed each word. "What did he say?"

Krish wasn't going to relent. So, I finally decided to open up, to share the truth that had been haunting me for so long. "Remember the day you shot Ron, the kingpin of the drug cartel, to save me in Kuala Lumpur?"

Krish recalled that action-packed scene vividly. Ron had been taking me away at gunpoint, heading towards a chopper that would have allowed him to escape. Even Ayaan had been defenceless in stopping him. Then Krish had arrived, making the split-second decision to shoot Ron and save me, even if it meant wiping out years of work in unravelling the other heads of the drug cartel.

"I woke up in the hospital," I continued, "and I learned from my team leader, Sudesh, that you had shot Ron to save me, that you had risked your own career for me. That was the moment I realised your love for me was greater than every force in this world, Krish. I had decided that I would stand by you no matter what and never let you go from my life. But that's when I got a call from your father."

I paused, the memory still fresh in my mind, the pain of that conversation etched into my heart. Krish's eyes were fixed on me, imploring me to continue. And I narrated the entire conversation that happened to him.

I was confused when Krish's father called me, but I still answered, trying to be as professional as possible. However, a lingering fear told me this wasn't a normal call to check in on me.

"Hello."

"Trisha Chaudhary?" he asked in a commanding voice.

"Yes, Sir," I replied.

"I have the reports of the mission, and I don't need to tell you I'm not impressed. It was an utter failure, in my opinion, with Ron dead."

"Sir, we still have some intel to start everything from scratch," I offered weakly.

"And waste the next two years looking for the other heads who worked for Ron in that drug cartel?" he snapped. "No, Miss Chaudhary. No matter how many excuses you give me now, this is still not going to work. None of this would have happened if I hadn't allowed Krish and you to work together on this mission. It's my fault, too, and I won't let myself go unpunished for it."

I was confused by his words, but he continued, "Do you love Krish?" The question caught me off guard. "Because I don't have to ask him if he loves you. His current action of killing Ron without thinking once about the mission and its success proved that. So, answer me, do you love Krish?"

I had remained silent about my feelings for Krish for so long, but this time, I replied without fear. "Yes, I do, Sir."

There was a long pause before his father began again. "Then what have you planned to do next? Leave the job, make Krish do the same and start a family?" He spoke as if it were the wrong choice. "Have you forgotten all the promises that you made to GLEN when you joined us? To serve this organisation for the rest of your lives?"

"I haven't forgotten any of those promises, Sir, and I still stick by them," I interrupted him. "Wanting to have a relationship with Krish doesn't mean we have to quit our roles in GLEN."

That's when he argued, "Your relationship is a liability, a weakness that could compromise your ability to do your job effectively. Both you and Krish. But if you still want to prove me wrong, then this is what I have to offer you, Trisha. So, listen carefully."

My heart was beating fast, dreading what he was going to say next.

"I give you two choices. Option one: for the failure of this mission, I would ground you forever from fieldwork, and you would be assigned only desk-based jobs henceforth. Not to mention, Krish will lose his Director role permanently at GLEN. Or option two: you get to continue your next missions, and Krish will only be suspended for a few months for his mistake. Now, the choice is yours. You select the first option, and you will have Krish, but you will ruin his career forever. Is that what you want?"

I felt frustrated and disappointed with the choices Krish's father was forcing me to consider.

"I know my son. If I gave him these options, he would still choose you, willing to lose his entire career for you. But Trisha, remember one thing. If you really love Krish, then you wouldn't destroy his efforts and hard work for years to be where he is today. I want him to take my role one day when I resign. All of these dreams will be shattered, and for what? Just because he loved a woman. I'm not saying love is wrong. You two can have a future, but right now, the state that you two are in, I don't think it's the right time to dwell on relationships. Krish needs to focus on his work, and being in love would distract him from that. Remember, great people are born by making great sacrifices. This is your only chance to show your greatness, Trisha. Let my son achieve the goals that he is so close to. Don't be a thorn in his way. I hope you will make the right choice."

I shivered as I shared this conversation with Krish, unable to control my tears for the first time. He shook me gently, his eyes boring into mine, shocked that his father could do all this.

"Your father gave me an ultimatum," I managed to choke out. "And you know what decision I took, Krish. I couldn't bear to strip you off from your Director's role forever."

Krish's expression hardened, his jaw clenching in anger, shock and disbelief. "He... he did that? He threatened you?"

I placed a trembling hand on his arm, trying to calm him. "Krish, please understand. Your father was only looking out for your best interests. He wanted to protect your future, your legacy."

"At the cost of our happiness?" Krish shot back. "At the cost of our love?"

I shook my head, the tears flowing freely now. "I didn't see it that way at the time. All I could think about was how much you had sacrificed to get to where you were, how close you were to achieving your dreams. I couldn't be the one to take that away from you, not when your father was right—our relationship could have compromised our ability to do our jobs effectively. I thought... I thought if I walked away, it would be easier for you to move on, to focus on your career without the distractions of our love."

Krish cupped my face in his hands, his touch gentle yet firm. "Don't you see, Trisha? None of that matters without you by my side.

You are my dream, my legacy. And if my father can't understand that, then it's his loss, not ours."

His words cut through the pain and self-doubt that had plagued me for so long. In that moment, I realised that I had been trying to protect Krish from the wrong thing. It wasn't our love that was his weakness; it was the fear of losing each other that had made us both vulnerable.

He stroked my hair gently, his own voice thick with emotion. "Why didn't you fight for us, Trisha? Why didn't you come to me with this?"

"I'm sorry, Krish," I whispered. "I'm sorry for letting your father's threats dictate our lives."

Krish pressed his forehead against mine, his breath warm on my face. I instantly slid my arms around his form and hugged him tight. He kept stroking my back as we both tried to understand and accept the turn of events that had torn us apart, leaving us with no other choices at the time.

"I need to speak to Dad in the morning. This is a serious issue, and I won't let him control our lives any longer," Krish muttered a while later.

I pulled away, shaking my head. "You wouldn't do anything like that," I said firmly.

"Why not?" he challenged. "I want to give this an end, Trisha."

"The only end to this is to keep continuing what we've been doing so far," I replied. "At least until our present mission is over."

Krish looked confused, so I explained further.

"Once again, you and I are working together. I'm guarding Meher's life, and you're assisting Ayaan against some mafia gang who is after the Shergills and Walias. We can't afford any mistakes this time, as this mission is more personal to us than just a job with Ayaan and Meher involved. I don't want our relationship to become a liability again, as your father once termed it."

Anger flashed in Krish's eyes. "You still want us to act like we don't want each other?"

I didn't want to, but that was the best thing to do for now. My silence gave Krish the answer he needed. And he wasn't convinced.

"You're still repeating the same old mistake, Trisha, of keeping an unnecessary distance," he said, his voice rising.

I knew I had to make him understand, so I pleaded a bit.

"Please, Krish. Try to understand what I am asking from you." I leaned in to press a soft kiss against his cheek.

"Don't," he said tightly, although his anger seemed to mellow a bit. But he still wasn't giving in to my demand. Emboldened, I kissed his other cheek, and that seemed to be the end of his patience.

In a sudden movement, Krish pulled me onto his lap on the couch. I gasped at the abrupt change in our positions.

"Stop kissing me like I'm a baby who could be appeased with kisses," he murmured, his voice deep and husky.

I couldn't help but grin at his teasing remark.

"If you act like a child, that's how I'll have to treat you. I can't think of any other way," I chuckled, but Krish's expression remained serious as he pulled me closer, our bodies pressed together intimately.

"Let me teach you the adult way of treating me, then," he said before claiming my lips in a burning kiss.

I kissed him back eagerly, instantly, shamelessly. Despite just telling him a minute ago that we should be maintaining some distance at least until our present mission was over, I still couldn't control my actions. My fingers tangled in his hair as the kiss deepened. His hands roamed over my body, deftly unbuttoning my tight shirt. He then dipped his head lower, trailing kisses along my collarbone and down to the swell of my breasts.

"No more doubts, Trisha," he murmured against my skin.

A soft moan escaped my lips as he lavished attention on my sensitive skin, his calloused fingers and lips tracing patterns in their wake. I arched into his touch, craving more, needing to feel the heat of his body against mine.

"No more fears," he added. "No more distance."

Without breaking our passionate embrace, Krish shifted us until I was lying beneath him on the couch, his weight deliciously pressing me into the cushions. He looked into my eyes, my lips already burning for his touch again.

"From this moment on, we face everything together, as partners, as soulmates. Nothing will ever tear us apart again."

His declaration bloomed something inside me. I clutched at his shirt, wanting to pull him to me, to kiss him senselessly for still loving me despite all my attempts to put distance between us.

"Say you agree, Trisha," he nibbled my earlobe, coaxing me further. "Say it."

I couldn't resist sliding my hands lower, grabbing his ass.

"I agree," I finally said, and the next instant, his body crushed into mine, his lips grazed every inch of my neck.

Though we were on the couch, with Ayaan or Meher likely to step out of the bedroom and catch us any moment, neither of us cared. I lost myself in the intensity of his kiss, my hands roaming over the hard planes of his back, revelling in the feel of his muscles rippling beneath my touch. I rocked my hips as he ground his lower body against me, giving me proof of how much turned on he was at the moment. Krish moved to my lips again, kissing me hungrily like he was starving for it all these years.

A sigh escaped me as Krish's fingers deftly unhooked my bra. I shivered as the cool air caressed my exposed skin. He trailed a blazing path of kisses down my neck, his tongue swirling over my pulse point before continuing lower.

I gasped as his mouth found my breast, his lips and tongue teasing the puckered peak until I was writhing beneath him, my body aching for more of his touch. Throughout my life, I'd never let any man get this close to me. It was only Krish, and it would be only him. My fingers found the hem of his shirt, and I tugged urgently, needing to feel the warmth of his skin against mine. Krish obliged, breaking our embrace just long enough to discard the offending garment before covering my body with his once more.

"I want you so bad," he mumbled before kissing my collarbone again.

With each caress, each kiss, the flames of desire burned brighter, our passion having simmered for far too long. When Krish's fingers slipped to the button of my jeans, I stiffened.

"We... can't," I told him, glancing at our surroundings once, and he realised it too.

We couldn't do anything like that out here in the open where anyone could catch us. Curbing his own desires to go ahead with this, Krish pulled away from me, offering me a hand to get up and sit next to him.

"Next time, we will take the bedroom," he joked, placing a kiss on my forehead.

"And what reason would you give to your friend for wanting a separate bedroom with his wife's bodyguard?" I teased, buttoning up.

Krish chuckled. "I wouldn't need to give any excuse. Ayaan would just know."

Krish slipped back into the shirt he had recently discarded and drew me into his arms. I planted another kiss on his cheek, then wrapped my arms around his waist, resting my head on his shoulder to calm my racing heart. While our night couldn't unfold as we had hoped, I felt relieved that we had addressed the lingering tension between us.

CHAPTER 18 (A NEW CHAPTER)

KRISH

I woke up to the sound of Ayaan entering the small kitchenette, his footsteps crossing the two-seater sofa where Trisha and I had spent the night cuddled in each other's arms. To make matters worse, Ayaan had also noticed the remnants of Trisha's lipstick on my cheek, raising his suspicions and teasing me about mine and Trisha's newfound closeness.

As my friend since school, part of me wanted to confide in Ayaan about my love for Trisha. However, given the risky situation with the looming threats from the Bat gang that Ayaan was coping with, I decided to keep this revelation to myself for the time being, at least until the mess was sorted out.

We had finally returned to the Shergill Mansion from the safe house now that it was deemed secure once again. Now, it was time to have an open conversation with my father about Trisha. What she had revealed to me last night about his role in our separation two years ago needed to be addressed. He was the one responsible for the pain and heartache we had endured, and I owed it to both Trisha and myself to get to the bottom of his actions.

With a deep breath, I initiated a video call to my father, who was currently in Austria.

"Hello, Dad," I greeted, trying to keep my voice steady.

"Good to see you, Krish," Dad replied, his tone cordial but tinged with formality. "How is everything going there? I heard you hired Trisha as Meher's bodyguard."

I couldn't help but smirk, my anger simmering just beneath the surface. "I didn't hire her. Ayaan did," I corrected him. "And she was his first choice because he believes in Trisha's abilities more than you do."

My father fell silent, waiting for me to finish.

"Now, don't act so innocent, Dad, that you have no idea what I'm talking about," I continued with bitterness in my voice.

"I don't need to act innocent," he replied evenly. "I just needed to act practical that day, and I did. It looks like Trisha has told you about the last conversation she and I had two years ago."

"Yes, she did," I confirmed, my jaw clenching. "And I'm shocked that my father could do something like this to me."

His expression remained impassive.

"I did all that as the president of GLEN, not your father. I see so much potential in you, Krish. I don't want you to let me down."

I felt my anger flare at his words. "So, for your dreams of seeing me in your position one day in the future, you are crushing my dreams of having a happily ever after with the woman I love?"

For the first time, I saw a flicker of remorse cross Dad's face as he tried to reason with me.

"Love is not enough, Krish. With love comes the responsibility to hold on to that love, and somehow it comes in our path of duty. Your mother and I had a love marriage too. But soon, she thought I was falling out of love, ever since I had to take up more responsibility at GLEN. But that was not true. I loved your mom deeply, she is the only woman I have ever loved and cared for."

He paused, his eyes glistening with unshed tears.

"Yes, I couldn't give her much of my time because of my duty. She was a housewife and kept waiting for me... days on end when I was away, handling and controlling these missions. She died... waiting for me, Krish. And you have no idea how I felt when she took her last breath, hoping I would come to see her before she died. And I... I tried, but I couldn't reach her on time."

Dad's words hit me hard, and I felt my own eyes moisten as I listened to the pain in his voice. He rarely spoke of Mom's passing, and the raw emotion he displayed now was a stark reminder of the sacrifices he had made for his duty.

After a moment, he composed himself and continued. "In your case, Trisha and you are both agents, and I don't want you two to fall out of love and keep waiting for each other like your mom waited for me."

I shook my head, "That's our choice, Dad, and our responsibility to see how we can find time to each other despite being away on missions. You didn't even give us a chance to reach that point in our lives where we can openly say to the world that we love each other. And I don't appreciate that."

Dad nodded, his expression painted with guilt. "I'm sorry, Krish. I did what I thought was best for you."

"Trisha is the best life partner for me, Dad," I countered, my voice thick with emotion. "If I'm with her, I'll have one less thing to worry about, one less regret about not having the person I love, one thing to feel motivated to succeed in life and in my duties too. You have to trust me, Dad. Trisha is my strength when she's with me. She'll be my weakness if you keep playing tricks like this to keep us apart."

Silence hung heavy between us as Dad absorbed my words. Then, he spoke, his voice barely above a whisper. "Don't hate me, son."

"That's your problem, Dad," I sighed, shaking my head. "You always presume. I can never hate you." A small smile tugged at the corners of my mouth. "I'm getting Trisha to Austria once the mission here is over. For your blessings, Dad. I hope I'm not expecting too much."

Relief washed over his features, and he nodded slowly. "I'll wait for you two."

Finally, after years of turmoil and heartache, my father accepted our relationship. I thanked him, and we spoke for a while longer before ending the call. As I sat back, I couldn't help but imagine the joy on Trisha's face when I would tell her the news — that my father had finally realised she was the one for me.

A weight lifted from my shoulders, a burden I had carried for far too long. No longer would we have to hide our love or fear the consequences of our choices. We were free to embrace our future together, side by side, partners in every sense of the word. Trisha was my everything, my reason for pushing forward, for striving to be the best version of myself. And with Dad's blessing, our love could finally take root and blossom.

I made my way to find Trisha in the living room. Tomorrow, Meher had to attend a family function of some of her extended relatives in South Bombay. Trisha was checking with the guards, instructing them of their duties and agenda for tomorrow to ensure Meher's safety. As I caught sight of her, radiant and beautiful, a smile graced my lips. In work mode, Trisha was nothing short of amazing.

TRISHA

Once the instructions were given, I dismissed the guards and turned around, only to see Krish walking by me. I recalled the promise we had made to each other — though we would continue fulfilling our duties, we were also serious about taking our love and relationship seriously. No more doubts, fears, or distance between us, as I had agreed with Krish.

I was about to approach him when Meher came over and handed me a box with a mischievous grin, and I raised an eyebrow in curiosity. Krish halted at a distance, not wanting to disturb us.

"What's this?" I asked, turning the box over in my hands.

"It's a traditional outfit," Meher replied, her eyes twinkling. "I want you to wear it for the function tomorrow."

"But why?" I questioned, perplexed by her request.

"Because I want you to," Meher stated matter-of-factly.

"But I'm not supposed to wear all this." I shook my head. "As your bodyguard, my duty is to remain vigilant and protect you at all times from any harm. I can't be celebrating with you at the event if that's what you want because one wrong move from me could have severe consequences. I can't risk that. Maybe some other time."

Meher frowned, then looked at Krish, who had stepped closer to us on hearing our conversation. "Krish, what kind of bodyguard have you hired for me who doesn't even listen to my commands?" she asked, a hint of teasing in her voice.

Krish chuckled, recognising her playful tone. "Did you obey the bodyguards your father hired for you in the past? If I remember correctly, you always gave them a tough time and eloped just to have some freedom from their constant following."

Meher bit her lip, acknowledging the truth in his words.

"So, Mrs. Meher Shergill, how can you expect them to listen to you now? And Trisha is right — wearing traditional outfits while she's on duty protecting you isn't a good choice. I won't approve of that; and don't even think of asking Ayaan, or he might not let you attend the function tomorrow."

Meher rolled her eyes, knowing Ayaan's protective instincts could indeed lead him to make such a decision. She smiled at Krish, trying to convince him instead.

"Come on, Krish. Can't you approve of such a simple favour for me? Besides, this function is safe. There will be Walia family guards too, and I promise I won't disturb Trisha there, except to show her off to my cousin brothers."

"What?" Krish scowled, clearly not happy about what she had said. "You would show off Trisha to your cousins? Why would you do that?"

Meher's innocent expression morphed into a mischievous grin.

"I like Trisha, and I really want her to stay close to me. What better than marrying her off to one of my cousins in the future?"

I was equally surprised by Meher's idea, though I couldn't help but feel a sense of warmth at her desire for me to remain close. However, the look of jealousy on Krish's face was priceless.

"If that's your plan, then I definitely wouldn't approve of this now," Krish stated firmly. "I don't want to lose Trisha to one of your cousins."

Meher furrowed her brows, trying to find the meaning behind his words. Krish instantly realised he had said too much. He quickly tried to explain himself.

"I mean, I'm not letting my best bodyguard, Trisha, be taken by one of your cousins. I need her... I mean, we... need her." He almost stammered by the time he completed saying that.

Meher burst out laughing at Krish's evident confusion and his attempts to backtrack.

"Fine," she conceded. "If you don't want me to do that, you'll let Trisha wear the traditional outfit I've gifted her. No more arguments over this."

With a wink in my direction, Meher made her way up the stairs, leaving Krish staring angrily in her wake. He then turned his gaze towards me.

"Why are you smiling now?" he scolded, noticing the grin on my face.

"You look cute when you're jealous, Director," I teased.

Krish sighed and shook his head, but a hint of a smile played on his lips.

"Wear the outfit... but... stay away from her cousins. You're mine... I don't want them anywhere near you."

I stifled a giggle before giving him a mock salute. "Yes, Sir."

Just then, Ayaan called out for Krish from another room, and Krish had to leave, but not without giving me another warning look to stay away from Meher's cousins. It was all in good fun, and I couldn't help but laugh at Krish's adorable display of jealousy.

The next day, I wore the beautiful traditional outfit Meher had gifted me—a lehnga choli with intricate embroidery and vibrant colours that complemented my skin tone. The choli was almost backless, something I hardly wore during my regular duty, which is why I couldn't wait to see Krish's reaction.

As I emerged from my room, ready for the function, I caught sight of Krish in the hallway. His eyes widened, and he seemed momentarily stunned as he took in my appearance.

"Trisha, you look..." he began, his voice trailing off as he struggled to find the right words.

"Like a woman that you wouldn't want to lose to Meher's cousins?" I finished for him, echoing his words from yesterday with a playful grin.

Krish chuckled and shook his head, but his gaze was fixed on me, desire evident in his eyes. "More like a woman I never want to let go of," he murmured, pulling me into his embrace.

I melted against him, revelling in the warmth and comfort of his arms.

"You don't have to worry about that," I assured him. "My heart belongs to you, and you alone."

Krish smiled and pressed a tender kiss to my forehead. Suddenly, his eyes twinkled with mischief. He trailed his fingers along the exposed skin of my back, where the choli I was wearing had a daring backless design.

"Why is this choli backless?" he murmured, his voice low and husky.

I shivered at his touch, feeling a spark of electricity between us. "What can I say? You should ask Meher that. She gifted me this outfit, and you even approved it."

Krish's eyes darkened with a mix of desire and playful jealousy. "Had I known that it was going to expose your sexy back to Meher's cousins out there, then I would never have approved."

Finding his possessiveness endearing, I couldn't resist leaning in and planting a quick kiss on his cheek.

"Don't worry," I whispered, "At our wedding, I'll give you the right to choose the outfit, and I wouldn't mind if you married me in my bodyguard suit."

Krish's eyes widened with surprise. "I can't believe you just talked about marriage," he murmured.

"Why? Haven't you?" I smiled, caressing his face tenderly.

A mischievous glint appeared in his eyes as he pulled me closer, our bodies pressed together intimately.

"Of course I have," he breathed, his lips brushing against mine. "In fact, I've even thought further than that..."

"Like?" I asked.

"Like what happens between us on our wedding night."

I couldn't help but laugh, patting his chest playfully to stop his teasing.

"You're incorrigible," I chided, though my heart swelled with love and anticipation.

Krish chuckled, the sound rumbling deep in his chest, and pulled me into a warm embrace, burying his face in the crook of my neck. We stood there, lost in each other's arms, until Meher's voice from the living room broke the spell. Not wanting her to see us like this, I pulled away.

"Stay alert at the event," Krish said, "Anything suspicious, inform me," he added before leading me out.

Meher met us in the living room, all ready to leave for the event. She looked me up and down, her eyes twinkling with approval. "I knew you'd look stunning in that outfit," she declared. "So, ready to meet my handsome cousins?"

I shot Meher a warning look, silently pleading with her not to push her luck. She merely winked at me, clearly enjoying the opportunity to rile Krish up. She definitely sensed something happening between us, just like Krish suspected Ayaan knew too. Just then, Ayaan walked into the living room, and Meher made his way to him, reaching him halfway.

Krish remained by my side, his hand finding its way to the small of my waist, a subtle reminder of his presence and his claim on me.

"You know," he murmured, his voice low and husky, "I believe I owe you a proper punishment for tormenting me throughout until you are back tonight from the event."

I raised an eyebrow, feigning innocence.

"Punishment? For what, exactly?"

Krish leaned in closer, his lips brushing against my ear as he whispered, "For tempting me with your beauty, for driving me wild with desire, and for constantly reminding me of how lucky I am to have you."

A shiver ran down my spine at the promise in his words, and I couldn't resist the urge to tease him further.

"And what did you have in mind, Director?"

His eyes darkened with a smoldering intensity that set my heart racing.

"Oh, I have a few ideas," he murmured, his fingers trailing along the exposed skin of my arm. "But you'll have to wait and see."

With a wink and a smirk, he turned and walked away, leaving me breathless with anticipation. Did Krish really meant what he just said?

CHAPTER 19 (ONE LOVE)
TRISHA

I felt a bit uncomfortable in the lehenga I was wearing. It had been years since I had worn such a traditional attire—the last time was during my own engagement ceremony, which now seemed like a lifetime ago. Life was good back then, but with Krish in my life now, it felt more meaningful and driven.

My eyes were fixed on Meher as she mingled with her relatives at the event we were attending in South Bombay. It was good to see her enjoying herself, especially given the escalating threats against the Shergill and Walia families recently. I scanned the lawn, ensuring Meher's other guards were in position before my attention was drawn to a group of young boys, a few years younger than me, openly admiring me.

I sighed and looked away, thinking, *'typical kids.'* That's when I recalled Meher's earlier teasing about showing me off to her cousins and an idea formed in my mind. Why not poke a little fun at Krish, who had been so adorably insecure about me wearing this lehenga to an event where I might catch the eye of other men?

Turning my back to the ogling boys, I took a selfie, deliberately angling the camera to capture them in the background, staring at my almost backless back. I playful pouted in the photo and quickly sent it to Krish with a message.

'I might have a fan club of boys here who want my attention. I didn't know traditional attire could make my charm irresistible not just to men but young boys too.'

I smiled, knowing his reaction wouldn't be good, and sure enough, my phone pinged with his reply moments later.

'Tell those boys to keep their eyes and their hands to themselves, or I'll have to teach them a lesson they won't forget. And as for your 'charm,' it's always been irresistible to me, no matter what you wear.'

I giggled at his cute, naughty, and jealous mix of a reply. Trust Krish to turn a teasing message into a possessive declaration of his feelings for me.

A while later, true to her word, Meher introduced me to her cousin brothers. As they flirted with me, exchanging harmless compliments, Meher couldn't resist teasing them back.

"You're lucky Trisha isn't in her bodyguard avatar right now," she quipped. "Otherwise, you'd have to watch out for her stunts and kicks."

We all shared a laugh at her joke, and I checked my phone to see if Krish had sent any further messages. Unfortunately, my mobile network connection was weak, and I had to ignore it for the time being, focusing instead on keeping a watchful eye on Meher as the event continued.

During a lull in the festivities, Meher sidled up to me, a mischievous glint in her eye. "So, Trisha, did you like any of my cousins yet?"

"Meher," I rolled my eyes playfully.

"What?" she grinned. "Don't tell me you need Krish's approval for that too. But besides, it's fun to see Krish all riled up and possessive over you."

"Well, I'm glad you find it amusing, but he is not possessive of me," I replied dryly, though I couldn't help but smile at the thought of Krish's adorable jealousy.

Meher nudged me conspiratorially. "Admit it, Trisha. He is. And you love it when he gets all worked up over you. It's cute."

I felt my cheeks flush slightly, but I couldn't deny the truth in her words. There was something undeniably endearing about Krish's protective instincts, even if they bordered on the irrational at times.

Before I could respond, another one of Meher's cousins approached us, his eyes fixed on me appreciatively. "Meher, you didn't tell me your friend was so beautiful," he said, flashing me a charming smile.

Meher grinned, clearly enjoying the opportunity to tease me further. "Ah, yes, this is Trisha. She's not just my friend, but also my bodyguard."

The cousin's eyebrows shot up in surprise. "A bodyguard? But she's so... delicate."

I couldn't resist the urge to play along, stepping closer to him and giving him my most intimidating glare. "Appearances can be deceiving," I said in a low, challenging tone.

The poor boy visibly gulped, and Meher burst into laughter at his discomfort. "I tried to warn you," she scolded her cousin playfully. "Trisha may look like a delicate flower, but she's a force to be reckoned with."

I winked at the flustered young man, unable to resist the urge to have a little fun at his expense. "Don't worry, I only unleash my 'stunts and kicks' on those who deserve it."

His cheeks flushed scarlet as he stammered out an apology, quickly making his retreat. Meher and I dissolved into a fit of giggles, drawing curious glances from those around us.

"You're terrible, Trisha," Meher chided, though her eyes sparkled with mirth.

I shrugged unapologetically.

"He should learn not to underestimate a woman, especially one trained in the art of combat."

Meher looped her arm through mine, her expression one of pure affection. "I'm so glad Ayaan hired you as my bodyguard. You're not just protecting me—you're keeping me entertained too."

As we rejoined the festivities, my phone buzzed with another message from Krish. I couldn't wait to share the details of our mischievous antics with him later, knowing he would find it both vexing and endearing. Such was the nature of our love—a perfect blend of playfulness, protectiveness, and an unbreakable bond that could weather any storm.

But the moment I opened the message, my heart skipped a beat. It was a red alert from Krish.

'Code Red. Get Meher back to Shergill Mansion.'

The instant I read it, I alerted the guards to prepare the vehicles. What was wrong? Why did Krish send that kind of an urgent message? I dialled his number, but the call wouldn't connect. Without creating chaos or drawing attention, I paced over to where Meher was chatting happily with her relatives and whispered that we had to leave immediately—it was a direct order from Krish himself.

Meher tensed beside me, but by now, she knew the protocol. She quickly informed her relatives about an urgency that had come up at home, and we would have to leave. I pulled her with me as the guards surrounded us, ushering us toward the cars.

"What happened?" Meher asked, panic lacing her voice. "Is Ayaan okay?"

"I don't know anything," I replied, my voice restless. "Just that Krish wants us back home. It's code red."

"What is code red?" she pressed as we hurried our pace to the parking area.

"Code red means a severe threat has been detected, and we need to evacuate immediately," I explained, my heart pounding in my chest.

We reached the cars only to find the tyres of both vehicles had been slashed, rendering them useless. Someone had done it deliberately to prevent our escape. I groaned in frustration before ordering the guards to arrange another vehicle as soon as possible.

That's when one of the guard's phones rang with an incoming call from Krish. He quickly passed it to me, and I answered, "We have a situation. The tyres are flat, and it looks like someone did it on purpose to keep us from leaving."

Krish's voice was tense but controlled.

"Wait for a few minutes. I'm already on my way, and I've sent an additional backup that will reach you in five minutes. Stay with Meher, and don't let her out of your sight."

I clutched Meher's arm tightly, scanning our surroundings for any potential threats as I disconnected the call. True to Krish's word, a team of additional guards arrived within five minutes, providing an extra layer of security.

Just a few minutes later, Krish's car pulled up, and he motioned for us to get in quickly. Meher slid into the backseat beside me, while one of the bodyguards took the front passenger seat beside Krish. Without wasting a second, he accelerated out of the parking lot, leaving the potential danger behind.

Once we were on the road and safe, I finally found my voice. "Krish, what's going on? Why the code red?"

His eyes met mine in the rearview mirror, his expression grave. "The Bat gang has been monitoring the Shergills and Walias movements, and they saw an opportunity today. We received a direct threat call from Raghav a while ago, and he knew Meher was here, and that Ayaan's father was at the Krida Udhyan attending the rally there to support Meher's father's campaign. Raghav might have planned a possible attack during the event there or here."

Meher gasped, her hand tightening around mine. "But how? We had security in place."

"They must have had inside information," Krish replied grimly. "Someone leaked the details of our security arrangements."

A chill ran down my spine at the realisation that they were making us dance like puppets to the tune of their threats.

"Where is Ayaan?" Meher asked in worry.

"At the Krida Udhyan to bring Kailash uncle back. And he has also warned Vishnu to stay vigilant around your father there," Krish replied, his jaw clenched.

The rest of the drive was filled with tense silence, with Krish manoeuvering the streets with expert precision, constantly vigilant for any potential threats. Finally, we arrived at the Shergill Mansion, where a team of GLEN agents was waiting to escort us inside.

It took a few more hours to handle the situation after reaching home safely. Ayaan had ensured his father's security, and now he and Krish were busy discussing how to end the threats from Raghav and his father, the Bat gang, once and for all. I remained with Meher until then.

Finally, after everyone had dispersed to their respective rooms, I headed toward mine, still clad in the traditional lehenga choli, waiting to undress. It had been a hectic day, and dealing with Raghav's mind games had been truly exhausting.

Before retiring, I decided to check on Krish first, as I really wanted to contribute in some way to the plan he and Ayaan had devised for their mission to capture the Bat gang. As an agent of GLEN, I wanted to be an active participant. Maybe if I showed enough interest, Krish might agree to let me join.

I made my way to his room and saw Ayaan coming out, carrying a file. Spotting me at the door, he smiled.

"Is Krish inside? I wanted to speak with him," I asked.

"He's in the bathroom," Ayaan replied. "But you can wait for him." He turned to leave but paused, adding, "Oh, and thanks for watching out for Meher today."

I shrugged. "That's my job."

"I know," he smiled back with a nod. "Get some rest, Trisha. You've earned it."

I nodded, thanking him. "Good night, Boss."

As Ayaan left, I debated whether to intervene now or come back later. Deciding to meet with Krish immediately, I barged into his room and shut the door behind me.

The moment the door click shut, Krish shouted from inside the bathroom.

"Ayaan, are you still there? If yes, pass me a towel, please. I forgot to take it."

I sighed, imagining how someone could forget to grab a towel before showering. Opening his closet, I fetched a towel and first locked the bedroom door, ensuring no one would see me inside. After all, we were in the Shergill Mansion, and our relationship was still a secret.

"Ayaan, don't tell me you didn't find that silly towel in my closet. You need to check your eyesight, buddy," Krish mocked from the bathroom.

I held back a chuckle, realising he had no idea it was me and not Ayaan in the room. Knocking softly on the bathroom door, I waited for him to extend his hand to grab the towel before playfully pulling it away.

"Ayaan, what the f*ck? I'm dripping wet here. Give me the towel. Play these tricks with your partner, not me," Krish groaned in frustration.

"I'm doing the same, Krish..." I replied, unable to resist teasing him further.

The moment he heard my voice, he peeked his head out from behind the bathroom door, his eyes gleaming with mischief as he laid eyes on me.

"What are you doing here?" he asked, a hint of surprise in his tone.

"I wanted to discuss something very important," I explained, handing him the towel. "Come out soon."

Instead of taking the towel, Krish grabbed my hand and pulled me toward the door. Surprised by his sudden move, I managed to shrug off his hold and pass him the towel.

"Krish, what are you doing? Come out soon. I want to get out of this dress too."

With a roguish grin, he shut the bathroom door, leaving me waiting for him in his room. I couldn't help but grin at his playfulness.

A few minutes later, the bathroom door opened, and Krish emerged, a towel wrapped loosely around his waist, beads of water glistening on his toned physique. My breath caught in my throat as I drank in the sight of him, desire pooling in my belly.

"Now, what was so important that you had to barge into my room?" he asked, his voice low and teasing as he closed the distance between us.

I opened my mouth to speak, but the words seemed to evaporate on my tongue as he drew nearer, his masculine scent and raw presence rendering me momentarily speechless.

Krish chuckled, clearly aware of the effect he was having on me. "Cat got your tongue, Agent Chaudhary?"

Regaining my composure, I swatted his arm playfully. "Don't be cocky, Director. I wanted to discuss my involvement in the upcoming mission against the Bat gang."

His expression sobered, and he nodded, understanding dawning in his eyes. "I see. And what did you have in mind?"

"I want to be an active participant," I stated firmly. "I'm not just Meher's bodyguard; I'm a trained GLEN agent. I can contribute, Krish. Let me help take down those who threatened our lives."

Krish regarded me silently for a moment, his brow furrowed in contemplation. Finally, he sighed, reaching out to tuck a stray strand of hair behind my ear.

"You know how I feel about putting you in harm's way, Trisha."

"And you know I'm more than capable of handling myself," I countered, leaning into his touch. "We're partners, Krish. In every sense of the word. Let me have your back on this, the way you've had mine."

He studied me intently, his eyes searching mine for any trace of doubt or hesitation. Finding none, he nodded slowly.

"Alright. We'll go over the details together and figure out how best to utilise your skills."

Relief and excitement coursed through me, and before I could stop myself, I flung my arms around his neck, pulling him into a fierce embrace.

"Thank you," I whispered, pressing a grateful kiss to the corner of his mouth.

Krish chuckled, his arms encircling my waist as he drew me closer. "You don't need to thank me. We're in this together, remember?"

I nodded as he looked at me and smiled again. "I, too, have something to tell you."

Krish cupped my face in his hands, his eyes shining with a depth of emotion that stole my breath away.

"I spoke to Dad about us and cleared everything up."

My eyes widened in shock. I had strictly told him not to tell his father yet.

"But Krish, why did you tell him?"

"Why not?" he asked. "I didn't want to wait any longer for him to know what a grave mistake he made by keeping us away, Trisha. Now he realises that you are the one for me," he murmured, his thumb tracing the curve of my cheekbone. "And he approves."

I was speechless. His father approved of us being in a relationship? That sorted almost everything that had kept us away so far.

"Once all this is over, I'm taking you to Austria to meet him officially as my partner. How about that?" he asked.

My heart swelled with the same all-consuming love I felt for this extraordinary man. Our lips met in a searing kiss as I searched for the perfect reply to give him.

Krish pulled me into his embrace, racing my heart while his eyes burned with want. I shivered at the feeling of his lips trailing along my collarbone, leaving a blazing path in their wake.

"Did you meet Meher's cousins at the event?" he murmured huskily, unhooking the strings of my choli one by one.

Even in a situation like this, where he was devouring my body, I knew how to rile him up.

"I did," I replied with a coy smile. "And I loved a few of them."

Krish's jaw clenched. I gasped as he undid the final hook, my choli hanging loose at the back. I instantly held it at my front, not letting it fall.

"You are mine, Trisha Choudhary. And I'm the only one you're allowed to love," Krish commanded before kissing me again.

His fiery kisses along my neck made my knees go weak.

"I was dying for this moment since morning…" he murmured, nuzzling his nose over my collarbone. "To help you out of this attire."

I froze, suddenly feeling very exposed. Sensing my hesitation, he tilted my chin up to meet his tender gaze.

"Hey, we don't have to do anything you don't want to," he said softly.

"I didn't freeze because you're undressing me," I began, leaning in closer to him, my voice dropped to a teasing whisper. "I froze because your towel has fallen down, and is now pooling at our feet, though I didn't look."

Krish's eyes widened in realisation, and he bit his lip, noticing his state of undress.

"Oops," he muttered, his cheeks tinged with a hint of embarrassment.

Then, a mischievous gleam lit up his eyes as he met my gaze, and I couldn't help but return his smile.

I leaned in teasingly, "You're at my mercy now, Director, and not vice versa," I added, diffusing the sudden tension with humour.

But before I could move and look away, giving him the time to dress up again, he cupped the back of my neck and looked intently into my eyes.

"I don't need your mercy, Trisha, I need your love."

His seductive words only inflamed the smouldering desire between us. Dropping my hands, I let my choli fall, baring my skin to his hungry gaze. I cupped his face and kissed him with everything I had, pouring out my passion. Soon, his mouth was mapping every inch of my tingling skin as I took the lead, guiding him backwards towards the bed.

By the time the backs of my legs hit the edge of the mattress, Krish had divested me of my lehenga as well. It pooled at my feet as he laid me down, nipping and stroking every tender plane and curve. Want grew into a desperate need as his hands and lips trailed along my body with unmistakable hunger. I craved more of his caresses, just like I needed air to breathe. His mouth feasted on every inch of my skin, but when he buried his tongue inside me, a swirling, all-consuming ecstasy overtook my body.

I'd never been this close, this exposed to any other man before, and having this moment with Krish, making love to him, I was awash with love, desire, trust and completeness. This went far beyond the physical—it was the deepest bonding of two souls.

"There's no going back after this," Krish said huskily, moving up and aligning himself over my body again. "Our missions can keep us apart physically, Trisha, but our hearts will stay connected forever."

"Always and forever," I replied in my haze, wanting him to continue.

Krish watched me with hooded eyes as I writhed beneath him for more friction of our bodies, until he could no longer delay entering me. The next few minutes were painful, but his kisses, his husky assurances that the pain would melt away, were all I needed to breathe normally again and continue moving our bodies together in perfect harmony. With every touch and every kiss, we explored the depths of our desire, reaching new heights of ecstasy together.

For the next few hours, the worries of the outside world faded away. It was just me and Krish in that dark cocoon of love and pleasure, our bodies united as one forever.

CHAPTER 20 (THE PROPOSAL)

TRISHA

<u>Two Weeks Later</u>

That passionate night with Krish two weeks ago kept replaying vividly in my mind. Finally, giving in to the burning desire that had been simmering between us for so long felt like stepping out in the sun after a long cold spell. It was a night that had changed everything between us, binding us together in ways words could never describe.

I remembered the way he had looked at me, his eyes dark with need and love. He had undressed me with such reverence, his touch igniting a fire that had been smouldering for far too long. Every kiss, every caress had felt like a promise, a declaration of what we meant to each other.

Giving myself to Krish felt like the most natural thing in the world. He was the only man who could touch me like that, make me feel so completely cherished and desired. As we came together, it was like everything else faded away, leaving just the two of us in a world of our own making.

His hands roamed my body with a possessiveness that made my breath hitch, and I basked in the sensation of being utterly his. "You're mine, Trisha," he had murmured against my skin, his lips leaving a trail of fire in their wake. "And I'm the only one you're allowed to love."

I had gasped at his words, feeling the truth of them deep within me before surrendering completely to him.

Just recalling the boundless passion of that night made my toes curl with longing. But reality had a way of intruding, and the very next day, we were thrust back into the chaos of our lives. The threat of the Bat gang loomed over us, and our time together became a rare and precious occurence for the last two weeks, until we had taken down the threat that hung over the Shergill and Walia families.

But when the intense ordeal with the Bat gang finally came to an end a week ago, a huge weight lifted from our shoulders. Ayaan and

Krish had masterfully orchestrated the entire operation to take down the dangerous criminals once and for all.

The car halted at the Mumbai International Airport, breaking my chain of thoughts, before I got down to board my flight to Kashmir. Yep! Just after the Shergill and Walia families were beginning to return to some semblance of normalcy, Ayaan whisked Meher away on a romantic honeymoon in Austria. With the two lovebirds off touring in Europe last night, Krish and I were left footloose and fancy free for a little rendezvous of our own.

So, under the guise of our separate "official breaks", Krish secretly planned an intimate getaway for just the two of us in the picturesque valley of Kashmir. Though our relationship was still under wraps from the rest of the team, this was our first real chance to enjoy the blossoming romance away from prying eyes. Until we boarded the flight, the secrecy of us travelling together had to be maintained. So, despite travelling together, we decided to meet directly inside the plane.

When I boarded the plane, looking for my seat, I finally saw him. Thankfully, Krish had booked our seats next to each other. In dark blue denim and a white shirt, with sleeves rolled up to his elbows, Krish looked effortlessly handsome, ready to seduce me with just his smile. I wondered how our one week together would unfold, if this was how he dressed and smiled at me — looking impeccably ravishing. Putting my luggage in the overhead compartment, I took my window seat and fastened the seatbelt.

"Why Kashmir?" I asked, turning to him as our elbows touched, already feeling the spark of the upcoming romantic times we were going to spend in each other's arms.

"This was my parents' honeymoon place," he replied with a grin. "In fact, I'm what you'd call a Kashmir honeymoon baby," he laughed with that teasing lilt in his voice that always made my heart flutter.

Leave it to Krish to make even the mushiest admission laced with humour.

"Is that so? Then I suppose we are heading to the right place to take this forward," I quipped back playfully, enjoying this rare opportunity to flirt shamelessly, without any distractions of our professional lives.

I swear the look in his eyes made me wonder if Krish was going to pull me over his lap and kiss me senselessly right then and there. He would have, if the flight attendant hadn't interrupted us, checking if we needed anything and diverting our attention.

We landed two hours later, and from the moment our car left the airport, I was awestruck by the pristine natural beauty that surrounded us—the towering snow-capped peaks, sprawling cedar forests, everything around was mesmerizing, like a dream. Krish squeezed my hand, his eyes twinkling. As the car drove higher into the mountains, Krish pointed out the window to the breathtaking vista of Himalayan peaks framed by wispy clouds.

"My mother always said this was her favourite view. She'd sit and admire it for hours."

I studied his familiar features, momentarily filled with a tenderness I hadn't quite expected.

"I can see why. It's... indescribably beautiful."

Our gazes locked, and I knew that I wasn't just referring to the scenery. A playful smile played across Krish's lips as he leaned closer until his face was just inches from mine.

"Almost as stunning as the vision sitting next to me," he murmured huskily, making my heart skip a beat.

And we kissed. Multiple times before our car halted at its destination.

Our private cottage at the luxurious mountain resort was something out of a fairytale postcard—rustic carved wood beams, plush Kashmir carpets, and best of all, a huge window that framed the soaring, snow-capped peaks outside. It was absolutely perfect.

We barely made it through the door before Krish captured me in his arms, his kisses searing with rekindled passion. He trailed his lips along the sensitive hollow beneath my ear, murmuring endearments that set my skin tingling with desire.

"You know, there are distinct advantages to this location being so remote," he said with a roguish grin. "The privacy allows for certain... athletic activities to keep agents like us fit, right?"

I grabbed double handfuls of his shirt and pulled him flush against me, delighting in the hardness of his body.

"Are you insinuating something scandalous?" I teased breathily.

His cocky smirk broadened wickedly. "When it comes to you, Ms. Choudhary, I'm always ready to get... athletic."

We collapsed onto the soft, inviting bed, a tangled mess of limbs and heated kisses. As Krish stripped me of my clothing, his lips traced every newly exposed inch of skin with fervent devotion until I writhed shamelessly beneath his touch.

"This is heaven," I managed to gasp out as he rained openmouthed kisses along my collarbone. "How could it possibly get better?"

Krish lifted his head, his eyes darkened to stormy jade with undisguised wanting. "Oh, I have a few ideas," was all he said before claiming my mouth in another searing kiss...

****

The next morning, I woke up cocooned in deliciously soft sheets, sunlight filtering through the gauzy curtains. As the heavenly scent of Kashmir roses wafted in from the garden, I felt Krish's arms tighten around my waist, pulling me back against the solid warmth of his bare chest.

"Good morning, beautiful," he murmured, his voice still husky with sleep as he nuzzled the crook of my neck. "Slept well?"

I hummed contentedly, "Like a log. Although I vaguely recall a certain someone thoroughly wearing me out last night with his... athletic pursuits."

Krish chuckled, the low rumble reverberating against my back. "Yes, well, I did promise a vigorous workout routine for this trip, did I not?"

Turning in his arms until we were face-to-face, I traced the chiselled line of his jaw tenderly. "And don't think I've forgotten about your vow to make me swoon at least once a day."

"A promise I am quite determined to keep," he assured me, though his eyes were sparkling with mirth. "That reminds me of a few specific techniques you mentioned wanting me to... re-visit this morning."

I felt my cheeks flush hot as his hand trailed slowly down my side. "Is that so? My, it's not even proper morning yet, and someone is getting naughty ideas."

"Only with you, baby," he purred, leaning in to capture my lips in a slow, smouldering kiss.

157

His tongue stroked against mine with delicious familiarity that ignited the slow burning of desire coiling low in my belly. I returned his kisses with abandon, savouring the heady combination of his warm, masculine taste and the crisp, fruity notes of the wine we'd shared somewhere in the middle of the night, still lingering between us.

We finally broke apart, foreheads resting together as we struggled to catch our breath.

"I never thought I would get so lucky, having you back in my life, this time forever," Krish rasped out, drawing me back into his arms.

I held him close as we watched the sun rise behind the snow-capped peaks, painting the sky in vivid shades of crimson and red. Life never seemed this perfect.

KRISH

It had been four months since the threat of the Bat gang was finally neutralised, and Ayaan and Meher's lives could return to normalcy. The moment Ayaan revealed his real profession as a Director at GLEN to his family, I decided it was time to open up to him about the depth of my feelings for Trisha.

The perfect opportunity arose during Devika's baby naming ceremony, with the entire Shergill and Walia clans in full attendance. I pulled Ayaan aside and confided my intention to propose to Trisha. I couldn't reveal that we'd been secretly dating for the past four months, but it was true that today I was going to propose to Trisha — for marriage, something even Trisha was not aware of. Seeing my best friend deliriously happy in his married life gave me the push I needed to seek the same joy with the woman I loved.

In the last four months, I had never broached the subject of taking that monumental next step. Today, I was finally going to ask for her hand — if she'd have me.

Ayaan gave me a thumbs up, adding with a teasing smirk, "She likes you enough to not say no, dude."

His vote of confidence helped settle the flock of nerves in my stomach. Still, I couldn't deny the kernel of doubt, that maybe Trisha wasn't ready for that level of commitment yet. Her role as an agent at GLEN mattered immensely to her. Would she still want the life of a spy if it meant being a wife too?

There was only one way to find out. Just before dinner, I took Trisha's hand and led her away from the crowd to a secluded courtyard nearby.

"Krish, what's going on?" she asked with a bemused smile as I turned to face her.

"Trisha..." I began, suddenly feeling like a lovesick teenager all over again as I gazed into her warm brown eyes. "These last few months with you have been... everything."

Her expression softened, but she remained silent, letting me gather my thoughts. I pressed on, "You know how deeply I love you. How important you are to my life now."

I drew in a fortifying breath.

"We've faced so much together, and every moment, good or bad, has only made me love you more."

She smiled, a soft blush colouring her cheeks. "Krish, you're making me blush. What's this all about?"

I took a deep breath, my hand trembling slightly as I reached for hers.

"Trisha, I know how much your role as a GLEN agent means to you. Your passion and dedication are part of what I love about you. I would never want to come between you and your work. But... I want to give a name to our relationship. I want the world to know that you are mine, and I am yours."

Her eyes widened in surprise as she realised where this was going. "Krish, are you...?"

I nodded, feeling my throat tighten. "I know we might have to stay apart sometimes because of our missions. But despite that, I want us to be a couple, a married couple. Trisha Choudhary, will you marry me?"

There was a moment of silence, and I could see the wheels turning in her mind. I was already afraid she might not be ready, that her dedication to her work would make her hesitant. She stared at me for a long moment, her mouth working soundlessly. A pit of dread formed in my stomach — maybe I had been too presumptuous after all. What if this was too much, too fast, and...?

"Krish," she began, her voice soft and thoughtful. "I never imagined you'd ask me this, especially not tonight."

Here it comes. I can't believe I've botched this so utterly... "Just think about it, at least? No pressure at all, I just —"

"Yes."

The single syllable cut through my panicked rambling, and my eyes shot to hers in disbelief.

"Yes?" I echoed dumbly.

She laughed, that bright, melodious sound that never failed to make my heart swell. "Yes, you idiot! Of course, I'll marry you!"

Before I could react, she flung herself into my arms, crushing her lips against mine in a searing kiss. I instantly melted into her touch, heady with giddy euphoria. While still kissing her raw and deep, I managed to take out the ring from my pocket and slid it onto her finger.

Trisha pulled away slightly, her eyes widening in surprise as she glanced at her hand. "Did you just put the ring on while we were kissing?"

I chuckled, feeling a bit sheepish. "I couldn't wait to put it on you, and I didn't want to stop the kiss, so I did it in the middle. You know how I can multitask," I winked.

She laughed again, louder this time, and threw her arms around my neck, hugging me fiercely. "You impossible, ridiculous, wonderful man..."

Holding her close, I murmured into the fragrant silk of her hair, "There's one more thing. Next week, we're going to Austria to meet my father. I can't wait for you to meet Dad and become an official part of the family."

She pulled back, beaming up at me with unguarded adoration shining in her eyes. "Neither can I. God, I love you so much."

"And I love you, too," I added, a touch of smug satisfaction creeping in my voice before claiming her lips once more.

****

Before flying to Austria, there was one more thing that needed to be done—Trisha was being relieved from her duty as Meher's personal bodyguard to take on more specialised missions, befitting her immense skill set.

I could tell it was an emotional parting for the two women, Meher and Trisha, who had grown incredibly close over the months they spent together, practically glued at the hip. Ayaan had already assigned another one of our top protective agents to take over for Trisha.

"Trisha, I'm going to miss having you around all the time," Meher said, her eyes glistening with unshed tears.

"I'll miss you too, Meher," Trisha replied, hugging her tightly. "But as they say, it's time for me to move on to new missions."

Meher sniffled and then smiled. "I'm happy you're joining the family once you and Krish get married. That's what matters the most."

I watched the two of them, feeling a mixture of pride and happiness. Trisha had become more than just a bodyguard to Meher; she was family now.

"By the way, Krish," Meher said, turning to me with a mischievous grin, "you saved me the trouble of matchmaking by finding your perfect partner yourself. I still have to look after two more—for Vishnu and Raghav."

My lips curved into a smug smile as I slipped an arm around Trisha's waist, pulling her closer. "Well, actually, Trisha was off-limits for other suitors even before she met you or Ayaan."

Meher and Ayaan both looked confused.

"What do you mean?" Ayaan asked, raising a brow.

"Well, when I first met Trisha, I fell for her almost instantly," I confessed. "We had a misunderstanding and broke off for two years. It was only thanks to Ayaan, who brought her back as your bodyguard that our relationship took a turn, and we sorted things out."

Ayaan crossed his arms, feigning anger. "How could you hide that from me, Krish?"

"Even I am a bit miffed you two didn't give me any hints about your previous romantic endeavours!" Meher added, but then her face softened into a warm smile. "But you two deserve this happiness more than anyone. I'm so glad you found your way back to each other."

"You might forgive him, Meher. I won't," Ayaan continued, his tone mock-serious. "Krish, I never expected you to hide things from me, especially something this important. I told you everything about Meher and me from day one!"

Meher rolled her eyes and turned to Trisha. "And here we thought only women couldn't keep anything in their stomachs and shared everything with their besties. Men are worse than us."

We all burst into laughter, the tension melting away as Ayaan bumped his fist on my chest, gently though.

"Dare you hide anything from me ever again," he warned.

"Never," I replied sincerely, giving him a tight hug. "Anyway, it's time. Trisha and I have a flight to catch to Austria so I can introduce her to our big boss… my dad."

"Yep. Say hi to Boss," Ayaan added. "I'll be working from here for some time, as he already knows. But you never know when work back there calls."

"Will miss you, buddy," I replied before saying our final goodbyes to them and heading out to the car.

The flight was long, but we were both in high spirits. This trip was more than just a visit; it was a chance to introduce Trisha to my father and solidify our future together.

TRISHA

As we landed in Austria and stepped out into the crisp mountain air, Krish turned to me and took my hand. "You ready for this?" he asked, his eyes shining with excitement and warmth.

I smiled, giving his hand a reassuring squeeze. "With you, always."

We arrived at his father's estate, a beautiful old manor nestled among the towering Alps. As we approached the imposing wooden doors, I felt a mix of nerves and anticipation flutter in my stomach. This was it—it was the second time I was going to meet the renowned man who headed the global agency GLEN I worked for. And who also happened to be my future father-in-law.

The doors swung open to reveal Krish's father. Even in his late 60s, he cut an impressive figure with his ramrod straight posture and intense gaze. This was clearly a man who commanded respect simply by entering a room.

Yet the moment his eyes landed on Krish, his stern expression melted into a warm smile. Father and son embraced tightly, sharing a look of obvious affection.

"It's wonderful to have you home again," he murmured gruffly.

Pulling back, he turned his assessing gaze on me. I fought not to shiver under his penetrating stare as he extended his hand.

"So, we finally meet again, Miss Trisha Choudhary," he said, his tone inscrutable.

I took his proffered hand, unsure if I should attempt to touch his feet as he was going to be my father-in-law soon. But I resist doing so for now. "The honour is all mine, Sir. Thank you for welcoming me into your home."

He studied me a moment longer before his lips quirked in a faint smile. "Please, call me Ratan. Any woman about to join this family deserves to use my first name or call me 'Dad'."

And just like that, the uncomfortable tension seemed to dissipate. Krish looped an arm around my waist, beaming proudly.

Over a scrumptious home-cooked meal, Ratan uncle indeed proved to be as larger-than-life and commanding as I'd suspected. He regaled us with stories from the earliest days of GLEN's formation, the gritty details of undercover operations that made my stomach churn. Yet he also shared amusing anecdotes about Krish's mischievous childhood that had me doubled over with laughter.

"He reprogrammed all the computer systems in the headquarters one day to play that ridiculous item song he loved those days, on loop!" Ratan uncle chuckled, shaking his head in fond exasperation. "It took our tech teams over a week to override his system hack!"

I shot Krish an incredulous look as he snickered unapologetically. "What? I was going through... a phase."

"More like causing me multiple headaches is what you were doing," his father retorted, though his eyes twinkled with unmistakable fatherly pride.

As the evening wound down, Ratan uncle turned to me with that same inscrutable mask once more. "Trisha, if you don't mind, I'd like to have a word with you in private before we retire for the night."

Krish stiffened almost subtly beside me, but I met his troubled gaze and gave him a reassuring nod. I knew he was worried after the last time his father had spoken to me privately as it had ended with him forcing us to go our separate ways. But I refused to let old fears and miscommunications haunt us any longer.

I followed Ratan uncle through the dimly lit corridors out to a serene courtyard terrace overlooking the snow-capped peaks beyond.

For a long while, we simply admired the view in silence, the tension building with every passing second.

Finally, he turned to face me fully, his expression softening into something almost paternal.

"Krish has already informed me of his intentions to make you his wife," Ratan uncle began gruffly. "I want to know — will you continue your work with GLEN after the marriage? Your skills are far too valuable to lose."

"Of course," I replied without hesitation. "GLEN and the life of an agent will always be my priority."

A ghost of a smile played across his weathered features. "I'm pleased to hear that. But I must also ask — will you give the same unwavering dedication to my son and your future marriage?"

I opened my mouth to respond, but he held up a hand to stop me.

"Please, let me explain. When you two were... involved before, I made the regrettable decision to interfere based on some misguided attempt to 'protect' my only son from potential heartbreak and make him focus only on his work."

He shook his head remorsefully. "It was a horrible misjudgment on my part, born of my own selfish fears. I'm sorry, Trisha, for everything that you and Krish had to endure because of me. What I failed to understand is that Krish is more than capable of balancing his commitment to this organisation with building a life with someone he loves."

Stepping closer, he grasped my hands tightly in his weathered ones. "You make my son happier and more grounded than I have ever seen. For that, you have my eternal gratitude and respect, Trisha."

My eyes burned with relieved tears at his words. "Thank you. You have no idea how much that means to me."

He gave my hands one final paternal squeeze before turning to look back towards the manor. Krish appeared, unable to stay away any longer.

His father turned to him, pulling him into a hug. "You have always made me proud, Krish. Now, I cannot wait to see how you both flourish in your love while continuing to work together at GLEN."

Krish looked at his father, his eyes shining with gratitude. "Thank you, Dad. I promise we won't let you down."

His father pulled away and looked at us both. "The wedding should take place next month, if you're both ready. After the wedding and a month for your honeymoon, I have a very critical mission awaiting the two of you. Are you ready for it?"

Krish and I exchanged a look, then nodded in unison. "We're always ready," we said together.

Ratan uncle's approving nod and answering smile were all the further blessings we needed.

"Good. Now, let's head back inside. We have much to prepare for."

Krish and I exchanged knowing glances, the corners of our lips quirking up in matching smiles. No matter what life threw our way, we were ready to face it head-on—as partners, as spies, and as a couple madly in love.

EPILOGUE (EUPHORIA)

KRISH

Ten months later

I stepped out of the monitoring van into the inky blackness of the abandoned Sandport Dockyard somewhere in Southern Africa. The cold coastal air carried a tinge of salt, and a vaguely ominous feeling seemed to permeate everything here. The dockyard was a sinister place, long abandoned and eerily silent, with shadows cast by the few flickering lights. It had once been a bustling hub but now served as a den for one of the most dangerous drug lords in the world. The remnants of old, rusted shipping containers and the skeletal frames of dilapidated buildings added to the foreboding atmosphere.

My eyes scanned the area, finally landing on the decrepit warehouse squatting in the distance. That was our target — the dilapidated headquarters where the nefarious drug lord known as *"El Sangre"* ran his vast underground empire. Despite his Spanish name, intelligence suggested El Sangre was originally from Thailand before expanding his illicit trade across multiple continents.

This sadistic individual was always one step ahead of us, operating his network in shadows through an impenetrable army of corrupt officials and merciless henchmen. El Sangre had been our white whale for months now, ever since we'd taken down the drug kingpins Ron and Aziz in Asia. But tonight, that would finally change.

Our sources from deep undercover indicated El Sangre himself would be overseeing a massive product shipment arriving here within the next few hours. It was the perfect opportunity to strike and sever the head of the legendary snake once and for all. Of course, given how repeatedly El Sangre had slipped through our grasp before, we weren't taking any chances.

I turned back to survey our tactical team assembled in the shadows. Highly trained GLEN operatives blended in seamlessly with the dockyard's shadowy infrastructure, weapons raised in silent readiness.

As I stepped out of the monitoring van, Ayaan's voice immediately crackled over the comms. "Are we set for tonight, Krish?"

Ayaan was in Manhattan, overseeing another critical mission. It had been a few months since we met now, but we were constantly on each other's speed dial whenever needed.

"We are set," I replied, turning to look at Raghav, Ayaan's twin brother, the once mafia who had worked alongside his father, Tej Khurana, notoriously known as "The Bishop" in the Bat gang. Raghav was standing against a car in his signature dark suit, with his hair gelled back. He looked like a broody, dashing devil, listening to music on his ear pods with his eyes closed.

"Though I'm not happy you involved Raghav in this op, Ayaan." I couldn't hide the irritation in my tone. "He could risk compromising everything."

There was a momentary pause before Ayaan responded with a hint of exasperation.

"Stop fretting like usual, Krish. We didn't have a choice."

I opened my mouth to protest, but Ayaan bulldozed on. "Raghav has been in this dark world ever since he was born, and South Africa is his second home. He has his deep connections here, and let's not forget if it hadn't been for his sources, we would never know that El Sangre is there."

Gritting my teeth, I had to admit he had a point. If it weren't for Raghav's underworld intel, we might never have tracked the vicious drug lord known as El Sangre to this remote dockyard. The man had proved insanely difficult to locate, always one maddening step ahead of us.

"Fine, I get your point," I sighed. "But that doesn't mean I have to like involving your shady twin in something this dangerous and high stakes."

I turned my gaze to Raghav again, who was still focused intently on whatever music was pounding through his ear pods.

"And what is it with him and this special music that he listens to every time?" I groused to Ayaan.

Ayaan let out a faint chuckle. "Not always. Only when he's really tense about a high-stakes op and needs to refocus his headspace before going in hot."

I rolled my eyes at that. Trust Raghav to be melodramatic to the core.

"So, you're becoming quite the expert on your newly found twin, huh? Good progress, man," I teased back.

"Raghav's still an impenetrable closed book in a lot of ways," Ayaan replied dryly. "But... I'm working on cracking the code, you could say."

I shook my head ruefully. Only Ayaan would keep steadfastly chipping away at that brick wall of a relationship until he made some sort of breakthrough. Then again, I was hardly the one to judge, given how long it took me to get through to the person currently occupying most of my thoughts. *My Trisha.*

"Is Trisha set to go?" Ayaan asked, cutting through my momentary reverie.

My gaze landed on her instantly as she stood off to the side with the team as she triple-checked her gear and com unit one final time. Her expression was eerily calm and focused, not a trace of fear showing despite the extreme danger she was about to put herself in.

I swallowed hard, worry gnawing at my gut. As always, I would never try to stop Trisha from charging headlong into the line of fire. Her determination and passion for this work were two of the reasons I loved her so fiercely. But that didn't make it any easier to watch her risk everything on missions like this.

"Yeah... yeah, she's ready," I managed to respond without letting the tension seep into my tone.

Memories of all the times Trisha had proven her incredible skill and bravery ran through my mind. She'd taken down countless criminals far more imposing than the scumbag El Sangre without so much as breaking a sweat. But I'd be lying if I said I wasn't just as awestruck by her sheer grit and drive as the first time I watched her in action.

"Krish? You still there?" Ayaan's voice broke into my thoughts.

I cleared my throat, shoving aside my lingering unease. Now wasn't the time. "Yeah, I'm here. Look, we'd better get this op underway before El Sangre gets a wind that something's up."

"Copy that. Good luck out there." There was a brief pause before he added in a slightly lower tone. "And Krish? Don't get too distracted by the lady, tough guy."

I couldn't help but chuckle at that as my gaze drifted back over to Trisha. "No promises, man. I'm only human, after all."

"And a husband now," Ayaan added, which brought a pleasing smile on my face.

Yes. A husband too. I married Trisha three months ago in Austria, and the very next day, we got this intel of El Sangre and started working on it, which meant we had no time for our honeymoon yet. The last three months, we hardly had time to even spend with each other. We both were focused on this deadly mission, which meant today, after all this was over, I would whisk her away for our honeymoon, having my wife all for myself.

"Call me once this is over," Ayaan said before ending the call.

I took a deep breath and made my way to Raghav first. He opened his eyes as I approached, pulling out one ear pod.

"Are we ready?" Raghav asked in a cold voice.

"As ready as we'll ever be," I replied, unable to hide my sarcasm. "Just make sure *you* don't get yourself killed."

"Don't worry about me. Worry about *your* team," he smirked knowingly.

"I always do," I muttered, turning as Trisha approached, her expression focused.

She joined Raghav and me, and I began to brief them once more, my voice low and intense.

"Raghav, your only part is to get Trisha inside, and once you spot the target—El Sangre—you will back off," I began, turning to Trisha. Her presence always brought a sense of calm and determination, and I needed that tonight.

Raghav was the key to this mission. He was the only one who had seen El Sangre before, back when he was involved in his father's illegal arms business. El Sangre had been a customer then, and Raghav's familiarity with him was our ticket inside this place.

Raghav nodded, his jaw set. A month ago, he had been tasked with contacting El Sangre's men, arranging a meeting under the guise of wanting to do more business with him. It was a ruse, a way to lure the drug lord into our trap so that we could finally take him down. Although he had refused to do this for GLEN, Ayaan convinced him, *somehow*, to use his underworld connections for the greater good of dismantling El Sangre's empire.

I then turned to Trisha.

"Once Raghav identifies the target, you will press the signal button, and our team will move in," I instructed her. "You'll personally take down El Sangre, and the rest of the team will handle his men."

I shifted my gaze back to Raghav. "As soon as you spot El Sangre and inform Trisha, your mission is over. You're out of there because if this fails, we don't want the drug lord's men coming after you for supporting us in taking down his empire."

Raghav pulled out an earpiece, slipping it into his pocket.

"Also because you're not allowed any weapons from us. In case the fireworks start inside, we don't want you unarmed and in danger."

A hint of pride played on Raghav's lips. "I don't need a weapon to save myself or kill my foes, Krish."

I silently agreed. The man was a beast, capable of taking down dozens with his mere muscle power. But Ayaan had been adamant — no weapons for Raghav in this mission. Why? I hardly got a chance to ask him that. Ayaan had brought Raghav into this mission. So, if that's what Ayaan wanted, I wouldn't refute, knowing he might have strong reasons for that.

"You're not allowed to kill anyone inside either," I reiterated firmly. "You're not a part of GLEN. You're a civilian now, Raghav, and we're not letting you take the law into your own hands. Leave that part to us."

Raghav let out an exasperated sigh, checking his watch. "Not interested either. How much more time to get in there? I've got a flight to catch back to India early morning."

"You're not being funny here, are you?" I retorted, trying to rein in my frustration.

"Having fun between jobs is Ayaan and your forte, not mine. I'm dead serious. Either we go in now, or I'm out of this."

I clenched my jaw, but Trisha stepped in, calming the tension that's bound to erupt. "The team is ready. We should go in."

Raghav nodded. "Good. Finish your pep talk then," he said before stepping away to give us some privacy.

"What the hell does he think of himself?" I snarled before Trisha turned to me.

"He's supporting us here. So, stop pushing him to the edge. We can't ruin this, Krish."

I tried to keep my anxiety at bay. She was right.

"Alright. Just be careful in there. El Sangre is not like the others we've dealt with."

"I know," she replied, her voice steady. "But we've come too far to fail now."

Trisha had always been the bravest among us, and tonight would be no different.

"Remember, we'll be watching your every move," I said, my voice softer. "If anything goes wrong, I'll be there."

She smiled, a brief but reassuring gesture. "I know."

With a final nod, I pulled her in for a quick kiss. It was a silent promise that I would be there no matter what.

I turned back to Raghav, who had resumed his brooding stance, turning back to us. "Let's get this over with," I said, more to myself than to him. "You know what to do."

Raghav smirked, a dangerous glint in his eyes. "I always do."

Ah! That pride! I watched as Trisha and Raghav disappeared into the shadows, making their way towards El Sangre's lair. My heart pounded in my chest, a mix of fear and pride swelling within me. We had rehearsed this plan a dozen times, but the real thing always had its own unpredictable edge.

TRISHA

El Sangre was my target tonight, and Raghav, the man who was once a mafia himself, was now the only one who could help me get inside the drug lord's den. A strange feeling washed over me as we neared the dilapidated building. I had worked with Ayaan back in Singapore, but working with Raghav was different — trusting a former criminal with a mission like this felt uneasy, even though he was on our side now.

Although I was nervous as I stepped inside El Sangre's lair, Raghav was completely poised, as if this were just another day on the job for him. We were stopped by the guards at the door, their eyes narrowing as they took me in.

"Who's the woman?" one of them growled, eyeing me up and down suspiciously.

Raghav responded smoothly. "She's with me."

The guard shook his head. "She can't go in with you to meet El Sangre."

Raghav's arm snaked around my waist, pulling me close. "She goes where I go."

I forced a grin at the guards, playing the part of Raghav's eye candy. The guard made a call, informing someone—presumably El Sangre—about the woman with Raghav. My heart raced. If El Sangre denied my entry, Raghav wouldn't be able to do anything, and our entire plan would be compromised.

While the guard was still on the phone, Raghav snatched it from him and spoke in an authoritative voice, the Spanish words rolling off his tongue smoothly. I had no idea what he said, but damn, the man had an attitude and a convincing power that could change even his adversaries' minds. He grinned, handing the phone back to the stunned guard, and without a word, he pulled me through to the next gate. The guard had understood that El Sangre had given permission for his woman to enter.

I let out a sigh of relief, but tensed again as we approached the next set of guards. The building was swarming with men, all securing the path to their boss. These guards stopped us, wanting to check for guns or ammunition. Raghav and I exchanged glances, allowing them to pat us down. I had hidden a knife carefully under the guise of a bracelet as no one would suspect it was a weapon.

They finished their checks and nodded us through, but one guard stopped me.

"Take off your ornaments too, including that bracelet."

My heart plummeted. If I removed the bracelet, I would have no weapon to kill El Sangre. I argued, refusing to take it off. When the guard tried to grab my arm angrily, Raghav lunged forward, punching him in the face.

"Don't touch my woman," he growled protectively, turning to me with an expression that said he didn't care about the consequences of my keeping the bracelet on. Right now, getting inside was the priority—how to kill El Sangre could be figured out later.

I agreed, throwing the bracelet off and walking in, chewing on the gum-like transmitter the entire time. These fools had no idea that the seemingly innocuous chewing gum was actually a soft device I would use to signal Krish and the team to storm in once El Sangre was down.

Raghav and I entered the dimly lit den, and he quietly pointed out El Sangre amidst a group of thugs and guards in front of us. We hadn't expected him to be surrounded like this—we thought he would be alone so I could take him down easily. Now, without a weapon and with all these guards, I would have to take them down manually, even if I signaled Krish and the team to come in.

El Sangre approached, saying something in Spanish to Raghav, looking seemingly happy to see him.

I murmured urgently, "You better greet El Sangre and make your exit, like to the washroom, so I can take them down one by one."

Before Raghav could respond, El Sangre was standing before us, his cold eyes appraising me. Raghav replied in Spanish, his arm tightening around my waist as he pulled me flush against him, playing the role of a possessive companion convincingly. I forced a sultry grin, acting the part.

El Sangre chuckled, a deep, unsettling sound. He said something else, and Raghav tensed beside me, his expression darkening.

"What did he say?" I whispered.

Raghav's jaw clenched. "He wants you to dance for him. For everyone."

"What?" I angrily retorted.

"That's what I promised him to get you inside," he muttered. "El Sangre has a thing for exotic dancers."

Damn this man!

"How could you?" I glared at Raghav, who shrugged.

"That was the only way in."

My stomach churned, but I knew I had to play along, at least for now.

"Any problem?" El Sangre asked as he looked between Raghav and me.

"No problem," I replied before faking a smile and turning to Raghav again. "Your part is done," I whispered, moving closer to him. "Get the hell out of here."

"One woman amidst a dozen vultures, and you think I would leave her alone?"

"Stick to the plan, Raghav."

"F*ck the plan!" he replied before pulling away from me.

Knowing El Sangre was waiting for me to begin, and I didn't want to give him or his men a chance to suspect us, I sashayed towards El Sangre, letting my hips sway exaggeratedly. His men hooted and hollered, their crude remarks making my skin crawl.

As I danced, my eyes scanned the room, looking for potential weapons, escape routes — anything that could give me an advantage. El Sangre watched me with a predatory gaze, his tongue darting out to lick his lips. I suppressed a shudder of revulsion, forcing myself to focus.

Then, an opportunity presented itself. El Sangre stepped too close, his hand reaching out to grope me. In a swift, practiced move, I grabbed his arm, twisted it behind his back, and using his body as a shield, I pulled the gun from his holster and shot him in the head.

Chaos erupted instantly as his lifeless body fell to the ground. The other guards raised their weapons. In that instant, I made my move. Pushing another guard aside, I fired at the nearest thug, then ducked behind an overturned table as bullets sprayed all around me. Out of the corner of my eye, I saw Raghav tense, hiding behind the pillar close to me. He looked ready to spring into action. Knowing there were men coming for Raghav from behind him, I threw my gun at him expecting him to seize the opportunity. It fell under his feet, and all he did was stare at it. He didn't pick it up. What the hell!

"Raghav!" I screamed over the chaos. "Pick the damn gun!"

Raghav's head whipped around, and a look passed between us — a silent communication that was so hard to decipher.

A bullet literally grazed my arm, but thankfully, it only left a bruise. I turned around to check on Raghav again, but he was a furious blur of movement by then, taking down man after man with ruthless efficiency. The gun was still lying down there, untouched. I immediately rolled to the floor, and taking back the gun, I shot a few more guards before tucking the chewing gum transmitter into my cheek, and I blew it, praying the signal got through to Krish. We needed backup... and fast.

The gunfire was deafening, the air choked with smoke. I picked off any man who came into my sights, but they just kept coming, like a relentless tide.

Then I heard it—the unmistakable sound of boots pounding against the ground. Krish and the team were here. A feral grin spread across my face. Krish and the others swarmed in, quickly disarming the rest of the men of the notorious drug lord El Sangre, whom I'd killed minutes ago. I did it! This was what I lived for—the thrill of the hunt, the satisfaction of justice served. And I couldn't wait for whatever came next.

KRISH

It was over! When me and my team took over the drug lord's den, El Sangre lay at Trisha's feet, cold and lifeless, his eyes wide open. She stood tall, her chest heaving, a look of grim satisfaction on her face. While our meticulously laid plans had veered off course, the mission was a success.

I didn't know if I had to thank Raghav for fighting in here and not leaving Trisha alone or to yell at him for changing the plan. But relief washed over me, as I rushed to Trisha's side, pulling her into a fierce hug. We had done it. El Sangre's reign of drug terror was finally at an end.

The future seemed a little brighter, a little more hopeful as we left that dark place behind us. And yet, I knew our work was never truly done. There would always be another El Sangre, another threat to face. But for now, we had won, and that was enough.

We reached the safe house, a quaint villa in South Africa that Trisha and I had all to ourselves for now. Tomorrow, we would be flying back to Austria to meet Dad and submit the report of this mission. Then, the very next week, we would finally go on the honeymoon we had been eagerly awaiting for.

It took us a few more hours to wrap everything up at the dockyard and take full control of the place. As promised, Raghav caught the next flight back to India, not wanting to stay involved any longer than he had to. Trisha told me how he had stayed behind to help her take down El Sangre's men, which relieved me and made me believe that he was indeed a changed man—someone we could start to trust.

Now, it was late evening, and Trisha emerged from the bathroom, freshly showered and wrapped in a robe. I waited with the first aid kit, ready to tend to the bruises she had sustained during the brutal fight inside the building just hours ago. Although the medic team had already treated her wounds, they needed further attention to soothe them properly.

"I'm fine, Krish," Trisha insisted, but I dragged her to the bed, making her sit.

"Those wounds need attention, and I'm going to help you," I said firmly.

She rolled her eyes. "They're just bruises, and they're not even painful anymore."

I didn't relent. Giving up, she lowered the robe from one shoulder, offering me a tempting view of her smooth skin that made my breath catch in my throat. As I dabbed a cotton ball onto her bruise, she stopped me, her fingers trailing along my face.

"No medicine can cure the ache, Krish," she murmured, her voice low and sultry. "But you... your lips, your touch..."

I clenched my jaw, trying to maintain my resolve. "Stop seducing me when you're wounded, at least."

She rolled her eyes again, pushing the medicine kit away before settling herself on my lap. My arms instinctively wrapped around her as she cupped my face and kissed me, her lips soft and insistent against mine. All thoughts of resistance melted away as I kissed her back, my fingers tangling in her damp hair.

Our kisses deepened, becoming hungry and desperate, as if we were trying to devour each other. Her robe slipped from her shoulders, baring her to me, and I trailed my lips along the delicate curve of her neck, savouring the taste of her skin.

"Krish," she breathed, her nails raking deliciously down my back. "I need you."

With a low growl, I flipped us over, pinning her beneath me on the bed. Her legs wrapped around my waist, drawing me closer. I untied her robe fully, taking in the beauty of her bare body, writhing beneath me, waiting for me to touch. There were a few bruises on her arm, her neck and one even on her abdomen from the previous fights she had in the missions, but they were part of her. And I loved her body, which was as perfect as the woman and the undercover agent she was. But these scars reminded me of something I had to tell her, and so I did.

"I spoke to Dad this morning," I said. Trisha pulled me closer as I continued, placing a hot kiss on my chest.

"And?" she asked.

"And I told him that you are going to be off the grid for two-three months."

She paused, kissing my chest and glared at me. "What?"

I grinned, expecting her to react the same way.

"Yes, Trisha. No assignments or missions for you for the next two to three months."

"Krish, stop making fun of me."

"I'm serious. I actually told him that, and he agreed. But of course, he would agree to this only if you want the same."

She visibly relaxed upon hearing that. "Thank god. I am telling him not to listen to your demands. There's no way I'm off missions for two to three months."

"Trisha, you have been taking up fieldwork back-to-back and it's taking a toll on your health. Take a break, recover, and then you can come back."

"No, I am absolutely fine. I can't think of a break that long. These missions are my lifeline."

"And what about your body? Your health?"

She was about to refute, but I didn't let her speak. "I want you to take this break, for me… for us… You can support all you want on GLEN's missions, but no fieldwork for some time. Please."

"You are worrying unnecessarily, Krish. I'm capable of handling the fieldwork."

"But your body needs rest."

"I don't think so."

"Fine," I sighed. "If you are not willing to give your body a break from fieldwork, then let's take a break from this…" I tried to pull away from her, but she didn't let me get away.

"What do you mean?" she asked.

"It's either you letting your body rest by not getting into fieldwork for two to three months, or I'll not over exert your remaining energy and tire your body by our lovemaking. Your body needs to heal and rest, Trisha. So it's up to you now. If you don't rest that way… then this has to take a pause."

Trisha groaned in anger and flipped me on the bed, sitting on me.

"Nice try, Krish. You know I cannot stop this between us… so I would eventually give in to your idea of taking a break from work."

I grinned.

"But none of this is happening. I want you as much as I want the fieldwork."

She unzipped my pants and pulled them down along with my boxers. Before I could even realise it, Trisha gave my hard member a gentle rub before gently sliding down on it, slowly, fully, taking me inside her completely. F*ck! It had been a while now since I was inside her like this. I gave myself over to my desire. I forgot everything I'd wanted from her and thrust inside her wet body, claiming what was mine. She rode me with all she'd got, our sounds of pleasure, pain, and relief echoing in the room. When it was all too much, I flipped her back on the bed and rammed so deep inside her that she'd feel me for days. She clutched my shoulders for dear life and watched me with her parted lips until she could no longer keep her eyes open. Her body tensed, and Trisha shuddered under me with a release of her own. I didn't last long, nor did I care. Seconds after her euphoria, white lightning exploded through my veins as I climaxed before laying my forehead on her shoulder to recover. Trisha was still recovering by the time I was ready for another round. I wanted to run my lips over every damn inch of her.

"I'm ready," she said with a smile.

"For round two?" I asked, my fingers dipping towards her wet core again while I was still inside her.

She pulled my face and kissed me hard.

"For a break, dammit," she replied in between the kiss.

She was ready for a break? I pulled away and looked at her.

"Are you sure?"

"I don't like to sit back and do nothing, Krish," she replied. "It reminds me of the time when I was shut out from my first job. That's why I haven't taken a break since I started working for GLEN. Missions after mission… kept me sane. But you are right. I need a break to heal and spend some time with you. Our relationship, our marriage, needs us to be together because these moments wouldn't come again the same way. So, yes, since you have already spoken to your father, and he is fine with it, I am going to accept and step back for a month or two. The only role I would like to play during this break is of your wife… your life partner."

I bent down and kissed her hard, allowing my tongue to graze with hers. I was glad Trisha had agreed to take this short much-needed break, and I silently promised to make the best use of it. I would show her the world, and fulfil all her fantasies. In that period, nothing else would matter — not the missions, not the danger we had faced, not the uncertainty that always loomed on the horizon. Just me and Trisha and the fierce, all-consuming love I felt for her.

THE END

Thanks for reading **'The Pursuit'.** Please don't forget to rate and review the same in Amazon. Your ratings and reviews matter to me.

For teasers / trailers and sneak peeks don't forget to check my Instagram Account @madhuritamse

For Bonus scenes/chapters of my published and upcoming books **Subscribe to my Newsletter-** https://madhuritamse.substack.com/

Amazon Books URL:

https://www.amazon.in/MadhuriTamse/e/B01MRJBSVD

Get in touch with me at any of the below:

Instagram: @Madhuritamse

Twitter: @Madhuri0302

MY OTHER BOOKS ON AMAZON

Scan the below Code and Click on the Amazon Link that pops up on your phone.

www.ingramcontent.com/pod-product-compliance
Lightning Source LLC
Chambersburg PA
CBHW031624170726
47990CB00017B/360